Crippled Fate

ANNA WALTON

ISBN 978-1-953223-17-3 (paperback)
ISBN 978-1-953223-26-5 (digital)

Rushmore Press LLC
1 800 460 9188
www.rushmorepress.com

Printed in the United States of America

For: Jared, Ally, Angie, and Addy

We love and miss you, Maxie Boy
March 10, 2009-May 21, 2019

Contents

There is no greater agony than bearing an untold story inside you

—Maya Angelou

Meet Erika Doss

It was time to wake up again and begin the day. Erika Doss laid there for a few moments before gaining full consciousness. As her eyes opened, she looked around the pale walls of her bedroom, her closet of disarray and piles of clothes that she still had no energy to sort through or discard. In the corner was Erika's jewelry box. The shelves sat half pulled out with piles of earrings scattered at its base. Erika rarely used the contents of the jewelry box. It seemed like each bracelet, each pair of earrings all reminded her of a world that was no longer hers, a professional world with structure, purpose, and prosperity.

As Erika sat up, her hands aimlessly wandered her sheets, searching for her phone. As usual, she read a text from a client changing their mind for the hundredth time despite having seen eighty-three homes over the course of six months. She felt a familiar pit in her stomach. It had returned despite the sun's optimism and the birds reminding her there is still beauty in the world. Erika didn't want to get up. She didn't want to repeat the same day she'd been living for the past three years. Erika was tired of trying. She was angry with life, angry with herself, and fully believed that any efforts she'd make to find financial stability and happiness would be in vain. Erika believed that despite having faith and positive thinking, there would always be people in this world who never find the happiness they seek. Erika wasn't looking for fame and fortune. She was in search of financial stability and a sense of accomplishment she felt she earned over the course of her life. She wanted to avoid chaos and turmoil. She wanted to avoid lawyers and court dates and people with blackened hearts. Mostly, Erika wanted to pay her bills without worry. She wanted a modest vacation once a year with her children, Luke and Evie.

Erika's heart belonged to her eighteen-year-old son Luke, twenty-year-old Evie, an amazing young woman she adopted many years before, and her ten-year-old faithful chocolate lab, Max. They were the reasons why Erika got up each morning. She'd given up on love after her divorce from Luke's dad. After a tumultuous affair and a failed marriage, she unanimously voted to swear off all romantic relationships, limiting her potential for future failure. She would never feel broken again, at least not by a man. As a younger woman, Erika was always in a relationship. She loved having someone to look forward to and to hold at the end of the day, but not anymore. Life has a way of closing a heart that's been broken too many times.

In late May this year, Erika had one less reason to get up each morning. This time, it was her beloved Max that broke her heart. Max was diagnosed with stage four bone cancer, just one day before Erika learned she had breast cancer. In the back of her mind, Erika thought her cancer was karma for having an affair several years ago, but she didn't spend too much time dwelling on herself. Caring for Max gave Erika a purpose as she dealt with her own illness. She didn't worry about herself. Her mission was to keep Max comfortable and with her for as long as she could. Doctors gave Max two to three weeks, but he stayed for over seven months. Max stayed for her, and while he was battling, Erika battled too. They fought together, and sometimes had their treatments on the same day. Erika spread a futon in the middle of the living room, and they'd rest together. Max reminded her he loved when he licked the palm of her hand and her touch, a scratch behind his ears gave him the extra comfort he needed. They understood each other without needing words to communicate. Max waited as long as he could before telling his mom it was time and she needed to let him go.

The night before Max's passing, Erika stayed up all night with her faithful companion.

She didn't want to waste a minute of her last hours with him. The family laughed at how loudly Max snored when he slept. This time, Erika recorded Max snoring. While she laughed as she recorded, his snoring, his breath, brought her much peace in the early days after he passed. Erika walked Max for the last time in the early morning. She captured a picture of the sun and the sky and she watched the clouds spread apart almost to say, "Welcome." Maybe behind those clouds hid Rainbow Bridge, Erika thought to herself. Erika watched Max saunter, much slower than his strolls in years prior. She looked up at the deep pink blossoms, showing off their beauty on the tree that has been bare, stale, and cold just days prior. Erika paused to ponder the symbolism.

Only a few hours later, Max took his final breath. Erika held her hand under his grey chin that told a story of a long life, well loved. She felt his last breath, and a deep emptiness emerged within. Erika wrapped her "Maxie baby" in her sweater with a photo of his family. His favorite crabby toy was tucked near his heart, and Erika said goodbye. She had held it together the best she could. Erika's heart ached each time she'd walk in and out of the garage. She could see Max using his last bit of energy to climb up the stairs back into their home after his walk. It felt so real, as if she were living the moment in real time. On the really rough nights, Erika was able to find calm with the sound of Max's recoded snore. She'd convince herself that Max was still there, waiting for her at the door. When morning came, it brought with it the cruel reality and her routine war of getting through the day began again.

Erika's cancer went into remission after three treatment cycles. Six months after her diagnosis, she was in remission. Erika felt guilty she'd survived cancer and didn't feel as grateful as she should. She knew many others who would give anything to trade places with her. When Erika was reminded of how lucky she was, she'd reply in kindness with a smile, but was secretly annoyed by their assumption. "Lucky" was the last word Erika would ever use to describe herself. She felt words as "cursed," "forgotten," and "insignificant" to be more accurate in reference to her current self. Erika thought she might feel more appreciative of "her gift of life," as Evie referred to it, had she really paid attention to what was happening with her. She regarded her illness as a mere annoyance, a hindrance to her time with her children and Max. Cancer had taken her beloved companion, but Erika had been spared, at least for now.

Erika didn't understand why she survived cancer when so many others hadn't. She questioned her purpose and what fate intended for her. Erika's obvious conclusion was that she was here to continue to support Luke and Evie, but was that it? Erika had lost her purpose in life. Once a confident and self-assured psychiatrist, Erika now found herself questioning and often trying to avoid every day. At age forty, she re-invented herself, now practicing real estate instead of medicine. Her finances were in ruins and she'd filed for bankruptcy. Erika loved her home of ten years. It was where she raised

Luke the majority of his life and where Evie came to share their lives seven years ago. This home offered Evie comfort and protection when her life was shattered, and memories brought only pain. Erika's home sat on an acre lot and offered Max a place to run and sprawl in the summer sun. Erika's sanctuary was gone now. She was restful that while her friends posted pictures and videos of their fortieth birthday celebrations on Facebook, she spent her fortieth packing up and moving from a home she never wanted to leave. Erika's house sold two days after her fortieth birthday, and she moved her family into a nearby condo. It did the job, but it wasn't home. The walls stayed bare, pictureless and bland, and empty, much like Erika.

With her life compass smashed, Erika felt helpless trying to set her life back on course. She hoped her real estate career would have stabilized by now, but there wasn't a single day she didn't worry about paying the bills and keeping up with Luke's pitching lessons. Erika expected the first year to be difficult, but now three years later, she struggled more than she had earlier on. Erika earned her real estate license while her medical practice imploded. One fall from grace and she lost everything. Life was unforgiving. She'd been a good doctor and sincerely cared about her patients. Sadly, caring was a liability. Erika had earned the respect of many prestigious colleagues and had a stellar reputation. Erika was real when real was rare and her patients trusted her because of it. Erika held no hierarchy of status, everyone was equal. She did what was in the best interest of her patients regardless of popular opinion and, sometimes, regardless of ethical mandates. Erika enjoyed pissing off the statutory "powers that be." She couldn't wait to leave boring Michigan, where she was born and raised. Even as a child, Erika disliked living in Michigan and instinctively knew there was so much more to see and experience. Erika paid close attention when she heard the singer Madonna attribute her success in part to her motivation to get the hell out of Michigan.

Luke and Evie were Erika's constants in life. She was a passionate and involved parent and was confident that had she not intervened in Evie's life when she had, Evie would not lead the healthy life she has now. Regardless of any monsoon that swirled over Erika's life, her children came first. She supported Evie's healing and Luke's ambition to play professional baseball. Luke was innately talented. He signed with LSU on a full ride, having spent weeks vacillating between LSU and Texas Tech. Luke's talent was nurtured by a mother with complete confidence in her son's abilities. In a few weeks, Luke would depart onto the next chapter of his life, playing college baseball and working towards a degree in marketing. Marketing was his "plan B." Everyone knew Luke was on track to be the next Chris Sale or Justin Verlander.

It was obvious that Erika loved being a mother and many wondered why Luke was her only biological child. Before she adopted Evie and while she was married, Erika responded to inquiries about her personal life, stating she wanted to invest her time into Luke and not spread herself too thin as a working mother. She wanted Luke to feel she was invested in him, otherwise he might grow up feeling insecure. Never did she ever want her secret affair to come out or that she'd gotten pregnant, suffered a miscarriage, and lost twin daughters. Nobody would ever know an adulterous miscarriage left her unable to bare children. Erika often wondered if people really believed her explanation. Anyone who knew Erika knew that she was all about parenting from afar.

Erika was a liberal parent. She allowed Luke, and even Evie, to make their own mistakes and believed the more she stayed back the more independent they'd become. She also knew the less invasive she was the more they'd trust her and confide in her with things that really mattered. Erika's parenting style was validated when Luke, sixteen years old at the time, called her as he ran barefoot in downtown Rochester. He left his shoes at a party when Rochester PD's finest arrived after neighbors reported a noise disturbance. She was the first person he called. As they laughed about the incident, Erika agreed that running from the cops was a thrill, but she sternly cautioned him not to make it a habit. Luke's dad criticized Erika for what she allowed him to get away with, but she held her ground as his parent. Luke trusted her to trust him and she did, he never gave her a reason not to. Erika treated many children who had strayed from their parents and she never wanted to be "that parent."

Luke was intelligent, strong, and athletic; he couldn't wait to take on the world. Luke liked to joke he would one day be Erika's retirement fund. While she laughed alongside, she was mortified. She didn't want her son to view her as a failure and feel like he had to take care of her. Erika wondered if Luke knew exactly why she lost her medical license. If he did, she hoped that he didn't secretly resent her or Evie for it. She hoped he understood some risks were worth taking for the right reasons.

Despite her extensive education, Erika was of the opinion that school was overrated and frequently took her kids out of school for a family vacation, back when she could afford the luxury of one. Erika referred to it as a "life experience" field trip and ignored educator concerns regarding absences. Erika knew from experience that life taught more than what could ever be written in text. Evie was no stranger to the painful realities of life. She and Erika met when Evie was thirteen years old, only days after she witnessed her mother's murder. Evie and her mother had been shopping the afternoon her mother was held at gunpoint. Evie watched in horror, her mind clustered with thoughts, and nothing made sense. A recent parolee executed Evie's mother as revenge for having been the presiding judge who sentenced him to prison over a decade ago. Evie became an orphan that afternoon. She had been an only child, her father passed before she was born, and there weren't any relatives available who were willing or able to take her in.

Plagued by grief and shock, Evie began to self-mutilate, convinced that she deserved punishment and karma for having caused her mother's death. Erika wanted to help the sweet, broken child in front of her. She wanted Evie to see that her mother's death wasn't her fault for insisting her mother take her shopping that tragic afternoon, but the fault of a psychopath out for revenge. Erika wanted to help provide Evie with clarity and insight and help her work through her horrific feelings, including the fear that her mother's assailant would one day seek her. Erika felt an unrelenting need to do more for this innocent child. She knew that she was meant to parent Evie.

Erika, heartbroken for the traumatized child, manipulated the system to allow her to transfer Evie's treatment to another psychiatrist. No longer acting as her doctor, Erika petitioned for temporary custody. If anyone were to find out that Erika had been her psychiatrist, she would face professional sanction. Back then, Erika had significant influence with the right people. She was soon able to adopt the young girl. Erika found that people never forget and vendettas last a lifetime. Favors from "powers that be" are much like selling a soul to the devil, there's always a price to pay. Years after the adoption, Erika's professional conduct underwent scrutiny resulting in temporary but severe professional sanction. "Let no good deed go unpunished," Erika often thought to herself. Still, she offered no apologies and would do it all over again if she had to. Erika only wished she could find her new calling or purpose in this world. She wished she would be released from her purgatory.

Luke and Erika had one main commonality—he loved to play baseball and she loved to watch him play. The first week of June was the kickoff to High School District Playoffs. Regardless of her poverty level, Erika never missed a game and balanced her busiest real estate month with her busiest baseball month. All Luke had to do was to look up from the pitcher's mound and he'd find his mother there, yelling loudly enough to piss off the other team. The field was Erika's happy place, the only "sanctuary" she had left. This was Luke's last year of high school baseball. Erika was saddened by the reality that should their team lose, it would be the end of Luke's high school baseball career; but if they won, it was onto regionals. Erika would miss high school ball, but she had his college baseball career to focus on now. Luke was moving on to bigger and better.

Erika had just gotten settled in her lounger, fully equipped with a leg rest and a cup holder when she heard a familiar voice call out to her, "Hey, Mama Bear." Erika bent her head backwards to see Evie's beautiful brown eyes dancing in the summer sun and hear her voice equally excited as she for the game to start.

"So, let's get this show on the road," Evie said as she plunked down next to Erika, chewing gum in a cowlike fashion. She made eye contact with Erika and they both laughed aloud, Evie fully aware that Erika was mortified by her lack of etiquette and short shorts that would catch the attention of any man with a pulse.

"Really?" Erika said with a disapproving tone.

"Really what, Mama Bear?" Evie asked with a bullshit grin on her face. "They're not that that bad. You're just jealous because you're fatty-floppy forty, and you have to Spanks your shit into place," Evie said while gasping for breath in between her laughter and her attempts at protecting herself from Erika's swat.

"Laugh now, Oh Wee One. Laugh now," Erika responded in a cautionary tone.

A wild pitch came thundering down into the fence in front of them and Evie couldn't resist an opportunity to razz Luke and was quick to yell out, "Um, you missed your spot, Little Boy Wonder. Don't suck today." In typical "brotherlike" fashion, Luke was just as quick to have the last word. He ran by her saying, "You better take your own advice, especially wearing those shorts that scream, *I'm desperate and need a boyfriend!*"

As Luke ran to the center of the field, he heard Evie's hysterical laughter and looked back to see her fist bump the air and tap her heart twice. Luke responded with the same gesture, offering a subtle smirk. Erika watched her children and felt proud to be their mother. Of course, she could have lived without their crude humor but in some ways, she was glad for it. They were carefree with each other and Erika loved that.

Despite their banter, Evie and Luke loved each other. Just days after Evie moved in, Luke came up with their secret gesture to remind Evie she was going to be okay and to reassure her that he had her back and he'd be there for her. After a while, Evie started to respond to his kindness with a smile and began repeating the gesture back to him. Evie didn't talk the first few weeks she was with them. Luke didn't know why this stranger was living in his home or about anything she'd witnessed. He just knew that something hurt the stranger staying in the room next to his, and he wanted her to feel safe and cared for.

For the next two and a half hours, Erika could escape from reality. She was with her two favorite people and nothing would upset or distract her. No sooner had she finished her pleasant thoughts, Evie called out, "Hey, Mitch." Mitchell Doss was Erika's ex-husband and Luke's father. Much like Erika, Mitch was involved in every aspect of Luke's life. He had been kind to Evie over the years. Erika filed for divorce around the same time that Evie came into their lives, and although he would never admit it, Mitch resented Evie. Before the divorce was final, he hoped for a reconciliation, but Erika had no intention of reconciling, regardless of Evie. Mitch wanted more of Erika's time than she was willing to give him by then. Instead of accepting himself as the cause, he blamed a broken child. Erika became indifferent towards Mitch. Their marriage had grown empty and she was done investing in an emotional sinkhole. Erika spent years dedicated to their family. She tried to be and act as Mitch expected, but it was never enough.

Years after their divorce, Mitch maintained he never wanted to divorce. He learned of Erika's affair, yet still wanted to work on their marriage. Mitch knew how lonely Erika had been. He knew all the times she laid awake crying, begging for him to talk to her. Looking back, Mitch didn't fault Erika for wanting out, he only wished he would have changed before it was too late.

She had done so much to help repair his relationship with his children from his first marriage.

Instead of showing thanks, Mitch and her stepchildren betrayed, lied to, and treated her poorly. Mitch had a tendency towards verbal abuse, was judgmental, and had been distant for many years. After numerous failed requests for marriage counseling, Erika had decided that she would seek therapy for herself.

Betrayal

Erika and Mitch remained friends after the divorce. When they divorced, Erika was self-sufficient and stable. She didn't ask nor did she want anything from him other than for him to be a good father to their son. Erika prided herself that she didn't need anything from him to make it. The first couple of years after the divorce were rough for Mitch. He was full of regret, but when he learned the details of Erika's affair, he urged her to report her therapist, but she never would.

Dr. Sean Collier was a big deal in the psychological community. He had a radio show and even a new book coming out, ironically, about marriage. It made perfect sense that Erika sought treatment from him. Erika and Dr. Collier had an instant connection. He was intrigued by her profession, being as it was similar to his. The relationship began as therapeutic, but it wasn't long before they'd meet for a drink or a casual lunch. Their first long adulterous encounter occurred in late October, a single kiss in his new Lexus. Erika hadn't felt anything exciting in a long time and he was intoxicating. Dr. Collier was older, grey, tall, and he had the "Richard Gere" look, something Erika could not resist. He had a single dimple in his right cheek that was paramount when he smiled. Erika fell quickly and was immediately infatuated with the charismatic doctor. What started off as a professional commonality and a sense of comfort and ease quickly turned black. Their relationship was erotic, sensual, and pleasure like she had never known. It was facilitated with secret encounters bated by lies and manipulation.

Erika was no fool to psychological ethical standards and knew the professional risk the charismatic author was taking. Any sexual relationship with a patient would very possibly result in permanent revocation of his license to practice psychology. Erika had been deprived of love and lust for so long, she was easily convinced if he were willing to take that type of risk that he would certainly leave his marriage to be with her. She was vulnerable, she believed everything he said. Only years later did Erika realized horribly he preyed on her. She came to him for help, but his focus wasn't on helping her, rather he focused on her long legs, as he'd later admit.

They spent the next Thanksgiving together in Chicago. A new world opened up for Erika. She was amazed at what his world of fancy restaurants and museums enough to put her into a trance. Somewhere along their travels, Mitch tailed them and hired an investigator to follow them. His intent wasn't to go after Erika. His intent was to inform the psychologist's wife of the affair, hoping to get Erika away from the scheming, sleazy doctor. Backed into a corner, Dr. Collier turned to threatening Erika to save himself. Out of fear alone, Erika decided to keep quiet and Dr. Collier walked away free and clear. His secret was kept, he completed his book, and moved on with his wife and his life. Erika learned of her pregnancy shortly thereafter. She was certain all the stress and the hurt of being so quickly discarded was enough to precipitate the miscarriage. Erika hemorrhaged horribly. She was lucky to be alive, but the miscarriage had done irreversible damage. She would never conceive again. Erika went to Dr. Collier for help, and as he remained safe and his life intact, Erika's life had shattered more than before she sought help from the seemingly respectable doctor. Most recently, Erika felt plagued by the sick irony that Dr. Collier destroyed her life in order to save his own, and she allowed her life to be destroyed in order to save another.

Mitch finished chatting with Evie and slipped a check to Erika. He had been good to her financially, especially in recent years. He always offered money and was kind enough to cover her monthly bills when she literally had nothing left. She glanced at the check and replied, "Oh my God, thank you so much. You have no idea how you just saved me." While Erika was grateful, she was embarrassed. Erika hated having to accept help from others. She borrowed money from every family member she had, including those much younger and less educated. Still, she was the one asking for help. Erika wondered how she could have allowed her life to tailspin. She was now in repair mode.

Lessons Learned

"Seriously!" Evie screamed, looking up from SnapChat long enough to notice that Ted was the home plate umpire. He was infamous for his ridiculously narrow strike zone, and every pitcher hated him calling the plate.

"This should be fun. Luke is going to lose his shit this game for sure. Doesn't this guy get that retirement is a good thing? Why can't he just go to Florida like everyone else his age? Go to the villages! Pick up a granny to make you happy so you can stop pissing off baseball pitchers and their families!"

Erika stared at Evie with a disapproving glare.

"You are going to get kicked out of this game if you don't watch it! He can hear you! He might be a cringy old man, but deaf he's not. Karma is going to find you, little missy! Be nasty, get nasty!"

Luke bent over, caught his breath for a moment and then positioned himself for the next pitch.

"Ball four. Take your base," Ump Ted yelled.

Evie could see the frustration on Luke's face. He rarely walked a batter, maybe one every couple of games. He had pitched a no hitter the game before. Erika and Mitch worried that this ump was going to get in Luke's head, especially calling four balls in a row with only the second batter in the top of the first. Evie saw Luke glance over at them, his jaw clenched and a stress scowl on his brow. She took the opportunity to reaffirm him with their secret gesture once again, but it didn't help.

"Take your base," Ump Ted called out again, this time louder, almost to rub it in.

Two walks in a row. That never happened. Even the other team was shocked as their whispers were easily heard amongst the crowd. Luke's coach took a minute to approach Ump Ted to see if Luke was hitting his spot. Their interaction quickly turned into a loud debate, and then into a full-blown screaming match.

"*Bam!* There it is!" Evie yelled as the coach was being tossed out of the game. "Knew that was going to happen," she said.

Evie looked at Erika with that maniacal look in her eye.

"Whatever you're going to do, don't," Erika cautioned, her warning falling on deaf ears.

"Watch this," Evie chuckled. "Excuse me, Blue," she said, catching his attention. "I think you may have had an accident," she said while pointing to his rear end.

Ted stopped, looked back to see if he had in fact defecated. He looked puzzled as his eyes returned to Evie while whispers and laughing soared across the field.

"Oh, I'm sorry," Evie declared. "I figured you're so full of shit that it would have to come out somewhere."

While the crowd roared, Evie began to pack up her stuff, well aware that her fate would be the same as the coach.

"You're outta here!" cried Ump Ted, mortified.

Evie smiled and replied, "That's the best thing that's happened to me all day!" "See ya, Mama Bear. Bye, Mitch," Evie said as she removed herself from the premises.

Erika said nothing and Mitch was too embarrassed to even look up. Luke, however, shot a smile out to his protector as if to say, "thank you." Evie left feeling proud as convoluted as that may be. Evie couldn't leave well enough alone. As she exited, she made sure Ump Ted, players and fans all saw her flip him off. Once Evie was out of sight, Ump Ted yelled, "Let's get this god-forsaken game over!"

"Why is she like that?" Mitch questioned Erika as if to critique her parenting.

"Probably because she's learned that life's a bitch and that you always look out for you and yours if you're going to make it in this world," Erika replied.

"So, you agree with what she just did?" he questioned her further.

"I think I do agree with her, actually. That ump is infamous for being an ass. Maybe it will deflate his head a little knowing that he might be called out. I do know I'm proud of her and I know that her brother felt loved. Back in the day, I would have loved it had you stood up for me like that, especially with your ungrateful offspring."

Mitch sat dumbfounded for a moment and responded, "Let's just watch the game. That's what we're here for."

"Of course!" Erika stated, knowing full well that Mitch hated the "would have-should haves" of their marriage and liked to avoid that kind of dialogue at all cost.

Surprisingly, Mitch became somber and humble.

"You're right. I should have had your back, especially with Elizabeth. You helped her and supported her more than most people do for their own children. She's a mess across the board, and I blame her mother for most of the mess she's become. Still, I could have done more as well to make her an accountable adult. I didn't though, and I'm sorry. As far as David, I don't know what happened there. He turned on me just the same. His mother taught both him and Elizabeth to have no regard for me, and look now, David's doing the same thing that his mother did with the babysitter years ago. We both accepted him for who he was. We supported his transgender surgery, encouraged, and praised him when he got his doctorate. There's nothing we could have done differently. I just think that he has too much blind allegiance for Elizabeth, and that's why he cut both of us out of his life. That was his decision and I've accepted it. They were very close as sisters and may have become even closer when he underwent all of his surgeries. I understand their bond, but he's only hurting her more by perpetuating her lunacy."

Now it was Erika's turn to be dumbfounded. "Thank you for that," she sincerely replied.

"Yep, anytime," Mitch replied in jest.

It had been a long-awaited moment of validation for Erika. Finally, they returned their attention back to the Luke.

Regardless of her lack of tact, Evie's intervention may have made an impact on cringy, old Ump Ted. Luke had thrown nine strike outs in a row after the first two batters walked. With an eight-point lead in the bottom of the ninth, it was clear that Luke would return to play another game next Saturday, then onto regionals. Luke was pumped and Erika was beside herself. Between Luke's win and Mitch's epiphany, she walked off the field of green feeling great, something she rarely experienced. Erika looked up at the sky and took a moment to breathe. The sun was warm. She felt at peace for a short-lived moment.

Evie had been laying out on the back of the car, tanning and counting how many expensive cars were in the lot versus crappy ones when her family returned.

"Freaking finally," she exclaimed as she jumped down from the car, kicking up dirt upon impact.

"So, Little Boy Wonder, did you kick ass?"

Grinning, Luke replied, "After you made that ump look like a little bitch, I did. I had nine strikeouts in a row!"

Elated, Evie jumped and hugged her brother.

"No way! See, that jerk just needed a reality check," she declared, proudly.

Mitch noticed Ump Ted just a car over, taking off his gear.

"You two need to shut your mouths," Mitch said, disgusted, but his efforts were in vain.

Ump Ted heard everything. "It's okay," he said, as he approached their car. "I already heard all you had to say."

"I'm sorry, sir," Luke quickly responded.

"I doubt it," he said in a solemn tone, shaking his head.

Luke felt horrible. He stared down, looking at the pile of dirt he was digging his cleat into. Evie began to speak but the umpire quickly put his hand up. It was absolutely clear that he didn't want to hear a word from her. Instead he spoke. "You were right, young lady."

Mitch and Erika stood next to Luke and Evie, now completely fixated on what the umpire had to say.

"I called those first few pitches in error. It appears they shouldn't have been walks. My wife had been fighting cancer for the past two years and she died four days ago. Today was my first day back in three weeks. I thought I was ready to come back, but I guess not. I swear I could still see her sitting out there watching the game. Our daughter played softball, so she was no stranger to a ball field," he said with a shimmer of a smile on his face, reminiscent of the happiness he'd had with her. "So, my point was that my eyes had teared up for a moment there, and my vision was blurred. I made the call the best I could right then, but my focus was on trying to hold it together and not cry. Crying would have been worse than being given the middle finger by a young lady who doesn't know her shorts are too small," he said seriously, with not even a flinch.

Mitch and Luke let out a snort that was intended to be a laugh, but both were met with contention from Erika. Evie was too mortified to hear Ump Ted's very honest and direct insult.

"Oh, sir," Evie said, her voice trembling and tears in her eyes. "I am so sorry, sir. I am so, so very sorry!"

"Young lady," Ump Ted began, "nobody likes to be made a fool of. Right or wrong. I know you were thinking of your brother, but you might want to look around you more and speak less."

Evie came and stood next to Erika, resting her chin on Erika's shoulder. Mitch hoped Evie learned a lesson and would at least try to be less impulsive. He also hoped her overly liberal mother took note of the damage her unruliness had caused.

"Young man," Ump Ted said, holding out his had to shake Luke's, "I apologize for the upset you probably felt at my poorly made calls. I hear you have a lot to look forward to in the years ahead of you. Honestly, you are one of the best pitchers I've come across in a long time."

"Thank you, sir," Luke began before being cut off. Ump Ted, now seeming much more vulnerable, halted Luke. Raising his hand once again, this time so Luke would make eye contact with him, said, "I'm not done."

Luke apologized and stood speechless.

"You're a great player but you aren't always going to be great. You will stink sometimes and there will be days where you won't be able to throw a turnip and hit a stop sign, but that's okay. Hold on to those days and learn from them. I've spent every day for the last seventy-two years being great and being awful. Believe it or not, it's the awful that makes you great. Remember that, son."

Luke wanted to lay a man hug on Ump Ted, but Erika's genuine hug beat him to it. Mitch stood, hands in his pockets, shaking his head in agreement with the lesson his son had just been taught.

"Thank you," Erika said, her hands almost a tourniquet around the elderly ump's neck.

Crippled

Luke loaded his bat bag in the car and was busy making plans for later that night when he heard Erika yell out the car window, "What's everyone looking for?" she asked.

Mitch and Evie headed back to their cars, along with Ump Ted, but now everyone was retracing their steps up and down the parking lot of the baseball field.

"Ump Ted lost his wedding ring," Evie yelled back.

Erika got out of the car and Luke hung up the phone so they could help Ump Ted's quest. He was growing increasingly panicked as he was now looking underneath vehicles in case it had rolled.

"I need to stop that bad habit!" Ump Ted declared. "This is the second time I lost it, fidgeting. I like to roll it around my finger you, know, but you'd think I'd learn from the first time," he added, still making the rolling motion with this finger.

"We'll find it, Ump, don't worry," Luke promised.

Luke spotted something across from them but couldn't make out what it was. He crouched down and was excited that the shiny item he had been unsure of, was in fact Ump Ted's wedding ring. Luke held it high above his head, "Got it!" he shouted.

"Luke, watch out!" Evie yelled, noticing the rear lights of a 2019 Ford F-150 truck that came barreling out without any warning. The two-ton truck backed over Luke, dragging him for almost a hundred feet before losing its grasp. People watched in horror and came running from every direction to help him. The driver, who looked about sixteen or seventeen, never looked back to check his surroundings and it was only after he felt the impact that he even stopped at all. Mitch went running to stop the vehicle, but the driver was not about to get caught. He sped through the parking lot, almost making Mitch his second victim before exiting, trying to make his getaway. Erika heard people yelling to "get his plate, get his plate," and she prayed someone had.

Erika and Mitch ran to Luke as multiple witnesses called 911. Erika didn't know what to do, he wasn't moving and his pulse was weak. Erika could see his extremities were severely mangled, and she began to feel faint. From the crowd, a man came running towards them. He was an OBGYN, but doctor nonetheless, and the father of one of Luke's teammates.

"Don't touch him!" the doctor yelled. "We need to stabilize him. We don't know what's broken and moving him may cause further damage. My name is Chris, I'm an MD. I'll stay with him until the ambulance get here," he assured them.

Erika was an MD, but she was paralyzed. Mitch was crying uncontrollably, hardly allowing Chris to check his vitals before demanding a status report. Sirens could be heard miles away.

"They're almost here!" Evie reported anxiously.

Ump Ted stood away from the mass of people. He wanted to stay out of the way and do the only thing he knew he could do to help the situation. He prayed. He begged God to take care of this bright young man and to heal him. Ump Ted began calling out the names of saints and the archangels, asking them to intervene on Luke's behalf. Whispers from the crowd began to follow suit as they called out for God's hand. The spontaneous vigil came to a stay as EMS and firetrucks approached.

Onlookers began to walk back to their cars, still in disbelief, in order to allow for room so the paramedics could work. Many continued to watch through their windows, hopeful to see signs of life. The area surrounding Luke was now silent except for the work of the paramedics. Chris spoke with the paramedics as they prepared Luke for transport, making sure his broken body was secure. Before they put Luke into the ambulance, one of the paramedics slowly removed Ump Ted's wedding ring that was still clutched in Luke's hand. He didn't have to ask whose it was, because as soon as he held it up, Ump Ted walked towards him to retrieve his ring. Amidst the muffled sounds around her, Erika heard the words "Eighteen-year-old male, significant trauma, pupils dilated and equal."

Erika clung to the word "equal" in her mind. "Equal, equal, equal," she said under her breath. "Equal is good." Erika picked herself up off the ground and rode in the ambulance with Luke. Mitch gathered Evie and drove behind them. Ump Ted followed as well, wedding band replaced once again on his ring finger, never to be spun again.

Erika was escorted through the hospital corridor as Luke was rushed into the emergency room followed by scores of medical professionals. She broke down on the shoulder of one of the nurses who tried reassuring her, but there was no consoling her. When Mitch and Evie arrived, the family was allowed privacy in a separate room outside the main lobby. Umpire Ted sat quietly in the main lobby, staring at his wedding band, thinking about the road ahead of Luke and the road he might have to leave behind, professional baseball. Ump Ted began to pray once and spoke out to his deceased bride, asking her to help the young man who was in such desperate need right now. Evie clung to Erika and Mitch sat alone by choice. He didn't want to be near Evie. Once again, as in the case of his failed marriage, he blamed Evie. Erika knew it too, but now was not the time to address his skewed thought process. It took all the strength she had to try and reassure Evie that Luke would be okay despite not believing it herself.

As she waited and time passed, Erika thought about her life as a whole. She thought about her loss, the betrayal, how she'd been preyed upon, and how she had been trying her best, transitioning to a new lifestyle so vastly different then what she once knew. She believed in God. She believed in a greater power, but she wasn't sure about reincarnation. Had she been a real asshole in a former life and this life was reparation for the one she lived before? Erika's heart was generous and kind, a fighter for the weak, and a protector of the young. Her thoughts kept circling and repeating themselves. Hours had gone by with no news. The family jumped when a nurse entered the door, but it was only because the police had arrived and they needed to interview all the witnesses. Erika made is very clear that she would not be speaking with anyone today and that her only focus was on Luke. If they wanted to talk to her, they'd have to do it another time. Convinced he would not change her mind, Mitch and Evie left to give a statement.

"Mrs. Doss," a soft-spoken doctor came in the room and sat next to Erika. "Should I wait for your husband?" she asked.

"No, no, no, no. He's my ex but no worries. Mitch will be a while yet, and I don't want my daughter to hear anything until I hear what you have to say," she replied. "Tell me, please."

"First off, I'm Dr. Langley. I'm one of the trauma doctors tending to your son. Luke started to gain consciousness while we were trying to stabilize him. He would most likely have drifted in and out, but he also had a seizure. I don't expect him to suffer long term with seizures but neurology has been called to consult. We'll have the information we need after that."

"Ms. Doss," she continued, "due to the level of trauma your son endured, the team and I felt it would be best to induce a medicinal coma. We gave him medicine to keep him under until we know the full extent of his injuries. We are running a lot of tests. My main concern is that he may have internal bleeding secondary to his osteopathic injuries. That being said, my impression is that your son is very lucky and is going to make it out of this okay, relatively speaking, that is, but we still have to wait and see before we will know for sure."

"I understand," Erika replied.

As she exited, Dr. Langley reassured Erika she'd return once she had better and more concrete information from the test results.

"I will be back to talk to you and the rest of your family," she said. "I know waiting is hard but honestly, this could have been so much worse. His vitals are strong. That's the best news you could ask for right now."

Erika heard the clunking of Evie's footsteps racing to return to where Erika sat. Mitch sauntered behind her much slower, keeping his distance, in a physical display of his upset with her.

We can breathe," she told them, "we can breathe." Evie sat and Mitch stood as both listened to everything Erika had to say.

Those first few hours felt like years. Erika finally relented and agreed to give the officer, who returned for a second time, her witness statement, but it didn't take long for Erika's anger to get the best of her. The more she spoke of the bastard, the less she could control herself.

"I want you to find the mother fucker who did this to my son," she demanded, her hands and teeth clinched in an effort to help control her rage. "Officer," she began, "look, I know that at the end of the day you are going to go home to your family and my son is going to be the furthest thing from your mind. He will become your Monday to-do list, and whether you find this poor excuse for a human being or not, your life really won't be affected. Unfortunately, sir, I don't have that luxury."

"Ms. Doss," the officer began in a casual manner, a manner that was apparently too casual because it set Erika off even more.

"Stop," Erika demanded, "Just stop," causing the officer's facial expression to go from sympathetic to angry. "Look, you're a cop, I get it. You're going to tell me about how committed you are to my son's case and all that other blah-blah bullshit. I really don't care about all that, to be honest. I just want you to find him and arrest him. That's all I want you to do. Please, go find him."

"Ms. Doss I am going to go now," the officer said, realizing that there was nothing he could say that Erika would care one bit about. She wouldn't care about his routine apologies or his promise to keep her updated about the case.

"I will be in touch, Ms. Doss."

"Thanks," she said as she walked away, not caring if she had been out of line.

Erika returned to the private room that they'd been occupying to hear Mitch arguing with Evie or rather at Evie. Evie sat looking down at her feet, tears dropping to her toes, as she held her head in her shaking hands. Her cheeks had lines of mascara down them, evidence of the pain she was feeling.

"Oh, don't you even," Erika said to Mitch.

He sat, angry, fiercely trying to explain his point to her about how this all started with what Evie had said to Ump Ted and had she just acted her age, that none of this would have happened.

"Mitch," she said, "I need you to go. I don't care where, but another end of the hospital sounds good right about now.

I need you to go so I can pick up the pieces of this poor child that you have just destroyed. You disgust me. You don't even realize that you just tried to shame and guilt my daughter for one of the most horrific experiences that could have ever happened to our family. We are all hurting, but unlike you, the rest of us have enough common sense to see that the only one to blame is the son of a bitch who hit Luke as if his life had no meaning."

"I do not care about her feelings," Mitch replied. "She's nothing to me."

Turning to Evie, Mitch looked at her and screamed, "You're nothing to me, nothing to my son. He's not your brother, and you're nothing more than my ex-wife's charity case. That's all you are."

"Security!" Erika screamed.

Looking back at Mitch, Erika warned, "Get out right now or I will have you escorted out."

Mitch left, yelling and reminding both Evie and Erika that he was "done with them," in which Erika simply replied, "God I hope so."

Evie was shattered. She had wondered how Mitch really felt about her over the years and now she knew. She never got a warm and fuzzy feeling from him. Their interactions, although pleasant, never felt sincere to her. Erika gently picked her up, sat her on her lap, and rocked her twenty-year-old Evie. Erika rested her head on Evie's shoulder, and she rocked her as much as the poor hospital chair would allow.

"I know you're crushed," Erika said. "What he said was cruel and uncalled for and there isn't any truth to it. Baby girl," she continued, "I need to you to be strong. I need you to understand that emotions are high right now. You can choose to get caught up in misdirected words from an empty man who is also a scared father or you can decide that you know better, as do I. Luke needs us. He is going to wake up with no understanding as to what happened. He is going to be afraid. A thousand emotions and fears will flood his mind, and he will start to panic. He is going to feel the worst physical and emotional pain, so much so that you can't even imagine. Now, baby girl, I know that you remember what it's like to be in shock like that. I know you know exactly what it's like to feel as if your whole world just ended and to have no idea what to do next. Luke is going to need you, of all people, to show him how to keep going. So, can you be strong for him, strong for me, and let go? That's the only way you'll be able to be the sister he needs you to be."

Evie wiped her face in her hands and arm, now covered in a mix of tears and snot. She tried to speak but couldn't and instead shook her yes. Her breathing began to slow down and her body started to relax.

"Thank you, Wee One," Erika replied. They sat for a moment, Evie still on Erika's lap. They were silent now and for a second or two, may have even dozed off. Both were numb and neither could completely tell the difference between a dream and reality right about now.

Dr. Fate

Mitch decided it would be best if he went home for a while and called Erika asking that she let him know when Luke could have visitors or if there was any news about the status of his condition. Erika didn't say anything about his earlier antics, she didn't have the energy and she was relieved he didn't try to defend his actions. Evie continued to sleep, now back in her own chair with her head propped up by a sweater she found in Erika's trunk. When Dr. Langley returned, Erika left Evie alone to sleep and followed the doctor to the ICU where Luke was now being treated. It was close to 4:00 a.m., and the kind physician was getting ready to leave but stayed long enough to share Luke's results.

"Well, as expected," she said smiling, bringing calm to Erika, "Luke's vital organs, his spinal column, brain, and heart are all perfectly fine. The seizure was a reaction to the trauma. Think of it as the brain itself, having its own panic attack. It's not common that we see a patient seize without having brain trauma or a history of epilepsy, but it's not uncommon either," she explained. "There are no signs of internal bleeding which is a miracle within itself. He'd begun to wake up on his own too, and that's always a great sign of normal brain activity. Still, we needed a complete picture of what we were dealing, so we induced coma. I really think you allowed us to do the right thing for him, Ms. Doss. Now that we know what we can expect, my colleague Dr. Kata will reverse the coma around 8:00 a.m. this morning." Erika fell back against the wall directly behind her, her hands clinched, covering her heart.

"Oh my God," Erika repeated. "Thank you, thank you, thank you." Erika said, sincerely staring at the doctor with eyes of pure gratitude. "So, what's next?" she asked.

Dr. Langley explained that Luke would be groggy and may take time to fully come out of the coma. Luke was allowed only one visitor at a time until otherwise directed, and Erika agreed she would be the best person to be with Luke when he woke. Dr. Langley cautioned Erika to prepare herself for Luke's immediate confusion and then his realization of what happened to him. She reiterated they had no way to predict Luke's reaction. Erika understood everything Dr. Langley was saying.

"Baseball," Erika said, acknowledging that she understood the point she was trying to make.

"Yes," the physician reaffirmed. "The damage done to his right hand and right leg is extensive. Very extensive," she said. "I've consulted with Dr. Benjamin. He's going to be in late this afternoon. He'd have been here sooner but he's coming in from Colorado. I'm sure he will be able to give you at least a preliminary prognosis and discuss the best plan of action."

"Okay," Erika replied and thanked her once again. Dr. Langley must have heard the skepticism in Erika voice or at least the pure sadness. She emphasized that Dr. Benjamin was world renown and one of the two best orthopedic surgeons in the country.

"Dr. Benjamin is licensed to practice in medicine in three different countries, so you're in good hands," Dr. Langley said. "They like him there too," she said smiling, as she approached Erika and offered a quick hug.

Erika had no choice but to trust Dr. Langley. All she could do was trust and pray. For the first time since riding in the ambulance, Erika was able to lay eyes on her Luke. She prepared herself for what she would see.

Erika slowly approached Luke's bed. His body was bandaged extensively, his broken limbs secured. He had a large gash under his left eye, surrounded by extensive bruising. Erika pulled up her chair and gently touched his face. Tears submerged her eyes and she allowed her body to relax enough so it would fold into a ball as she sobbed. With her head bent down towards her stomach, supported by her palm on her forehead, she released what seemed to be a tsunami of pain. In the background, Erika heard the beeping of machines hooked up to her son. Her focus was distracted by the ticking of the clock and the smell of antiseptic that permeated the room. Erika found the strength to come close to Luke once again. The events of the day replayed in her mind, and she blamed herself, certain that she could have done more to prevent Luke's pain. She should have been looking out for him, she thought. She should have seen that someone was in the car. For a brief moment, Erika questioned if Mitch was right about Evie. She quickly dismissed the idea, realizing that the ridiculousness of his accusation, and she wasn't going to let her judgment be manipulated by her heartache and fear. Erika prayed again. She pleaded for Luke to be healed and she prayed that she would be able to hold her shit together in front of him when he woke. Angry, she reminded God of all of her hardships and personal loss, all of her anguish, humiliation, and now, tragedy. She was filled with emotion and had no idea what to do with it. Erika demanded a sign from God that everything would be all right but, the confirmation she sought never came. Or did it?

"Excuse me, Mrs. Doss, I presume?" came a voice from the doorway. As she turned to meet the voice, she heard him introduce himself. "I'm Dr. Alex Benjamin" he said.

Erika wiped her face in her arm after searching unsuccessfully for a tissue, as she stood up to greet the new doctor. He came into the light and that was the first moment she felt something move within her. She couldn't define what she felt. It was strong and erotic. The sensation caught her by surprise and her mind spun in utter confusion. Erika hadn't felt anything move inside her like that and at a time like this no less. She, too, had caught the surgeon by surprise.

"Erika James?" he questioned; the words finally able to leave his mouth.

Erika gasped.

"Whaaaattttt? AJ?"

Laughing, he reached out and embraced her. "Hello, Erika James," he said, repeating her name for the second time.

Erika never enjoyed hearing her name as much as she did when it left the lips of the stimulating surgeon. Their embrace was strong and alluring to her. He was so different than how she remembered him. As she pulled away from their embrace, she tried to regain her composure but instead, she stood in front of him, dumbfounded. Erika looked up to at the six-foot-three beautiful man in front of her. His eyes were the lightest blue she had ever seen, almost translucent. His face was perfectly sculpted but clearly underestimated until he smiled. It was a face to get lost in and Erika was. He was beautiful.

"Are you okay?" he asked in a half-laughing tone.

"I'm sorry," she said. "This has been the most unusual day with the most unexpected events and more emotional upheaval than I ever knew was possible. Forgive me for literally not knowing what is happening around me," she apologized.

"You're perfectly fine," he said with validation.

Erika had known Alex Benjamin, or AJ, as she knew him as, since their second year as an undergraduate at Ohio State. He caught her intention when he dared to debate her on the topic of adolescent evolutionary psychology. Their first interaction ended with Erika threatening to poke his eyes out with the same small fingers she used to pick berries for her man. AJ's position was that the female's fingers were smaller so men could hunt and the women would gather. He was instantly amused by her feisty and passionate nature. She was less amused, decided he was a jackass with a Napoleon complex and didn't think twice about him after that. It wasn't for another two years until their paths would cross again, but this time at the University of Michigan. Much like before, he typically sat a few seats away from her in their first med school seminar. She made it a point to avoid him, convinced that he was nothing but trouble, and he had made it a point to get under her skin as much as possible. As fate would have it, they became inseparable friends.

Erika could never resist a dare, at least not when she was twenty-two, and AJ couldn't resist an opportunity to taunt her. The topic was once again focused on the physiological development of the female versus male skeletal system. AJ explained to the class how the male's phalanges were better developed and stronger than the female's. He could see Erika chomping at the bit to counter his stance, but she wasn't going to until he wrote, "I dare you to do it" on a sticky note and passed it to her. Erika's hand shot straight up, and it was on. After almost fifteen minutes of nonstop back and forth, their professor finally forced a truce. Erika was lit and AJ was once again amused. He won her friendship by relinquishing his stance at their next class, subsequently conceding to Erika. Now he had caught her attention. They spent their med school days working together versus working against each other. AJ fell in love with her but he never showed it and would never tell her. He knew she wasn't interested. A very late bloomer, AJ stood three inches shorter than her, and he was permanently friend zoned. He was her best friend and her confidant. Erika always had a boyfriend, and he was always her voice of reason whenever she needed dating advice. Once Mitch entered her life, AJ slowly faded out. After medical school, each went into vastly different areas of medicine and led vastly different lives.

As if she had just woken up from her own coma, Erika came to, looked at him, and said, "What the crap, AJ. When did you get so damn tall? You had to have grown about nine or ten inches in your twenties!" she exclaimed. "See, I told you chicks had superior bone structure, but you were like 'nooooo, men blah-blah-blah' and all that other BS you said," she laughed.

"Ahhh, that's the Erika James I remember," he said with a grin, taking the opportunity to go in for one more quick hug, but this one included skin to skin contact.

"Erika Doss," she replied.

"Oh, Rik, you didn't—wait, you did, you married Mitch, didn't you? Whhhyyy!" he nudged at her.

Erika shrugged.

"Let's just say it's been an interesting life and I want a mulligan for every one of my poor decisions," she said, feeling disappointed with herself. "We've been divorced now for several years but it's civil, well at least it was up until a few hours ago," she said rolling her eyes, thinking back to Mitch's nasty bitch fest and blame game with Evie.

Erika turned to her sweet Luke, waiting so patiently to wake up and tears filled her eyes again. "This guy, though, this guy is the best thing I ever did. I would go through every bullshit bad decision I ever made all over again as long as I could have this kid right here," she said gently, touching Luke's shoulder.

The same confused look quickly returned to Erika's face once again. "Wait," she said, "what are you doing here now?"

It had dawned on Erika that it was 5:00 a.m. and Dr. Langley had told her to expect him later that afternoon.

"Honestly, I don't know," he began. "I had talked to the ER docs and Dr. Langley at length about Luke, but what they were explaining to me didn't really match what I was seeing from the scans and x-rays they took. So, like I said, I couldn't tell you why, but something propelled me to see if there was an earlier flight and there was, so here I am," he said.

"Well, I am so happy to see you, J of A-ness," calling him another nickname she had for him in their younger years. "You have no idea how glad I am to see you."

"Me too," J of A-ness replied, shoulder bumping Erika. "Look who has to bend down now to reach your shoulder, huh?" he said in an attempt to make her smile.

"Yeah, yeah," she replied. "Glad to see you're still full of yourself," Erika countered.

Dr. Benjamin walked with Erika to retrieve Evie. Erika wanted her to meet him and also for her to have some time with Luke. Dr. Benjamin wanted to do an overview of Luke while he was still unconscious and take a second look at his records, hoping to clear up some questions he had.

Awakening

Evie was just waking up when Erika and Dr. Benjamin approached her.

"Hey, Wee One, I want you to meet someone. This is Dr. Alex Benjamin," Erika began. "He's an orthopedic surgeon and he's going to help Luke," Erika reassured.

Looking at AJ, Erika said, "Alex, you originally introduced yourself as Alex when you came into the room. Is that what you go by now?" she asked. "Is that what you want me to call you?"

"Yes," he replied, "Everyone calls me Alex, but no, I want you to call me AJ, or J of A-ness, or whatever the hell it is that you say." He laughed.

Evie finally fully awake, asked, "Um, did I miss something here?" she asked.

"AJ and I went to med school together," Erika replied, "we are very lucky to have him here for Luke. He just flew in from Colorado."

"Wow," she replied, "that's great. Thank you."

AJ returned a smile to the young lady and then asked if she wanted to sit with her brother for a bit.

"I honestly don't know what to think or say or anything, but yeah, I really want to see Luke," she told him.

Before she departed with Dr. Benjamin, Evie sat for a few minutes with her mother so she could get caught up on what was happening with her brother.

Dr. Benjamin looked at Erika and said, "You sleep. I'm going to get Evie settled and then spend some time looking at Luke's records before I check in on him."

Dr. Benjamin recommended that Erika call anyone who wanted to be at the hospital when Luke was brought out of his coma and reinforced that the only person allowed in the room would be her. Dr. Benjamin got a message that Dr. Kata was running behind so their consultation with Luke changed from 8:00 a.m. to 10:00 a.m. Still, in only a few short hours, Luke would regain consciousness. Erika couldn't wait to get her son back, and despite his behavior, she called Mitch to let him know what was happening. Afterwards, Erika took advantage of the few minutes she had to rest.

Dr. Benjamin led Evie to Luke and was surprised when he received angst.

"Now is not the time to try and get in my mom's pants, Doc, just so you know."

"What? Seriously," he asked, "what would make you think that was even a goal of mine?" He laughed before realizing that Evie was serious.

"It doesn't matter anyway," she continued. "My mom is like a no-fly zone and she shoots down anything unwelcome invading her space."

In a more serious tone now, Dr. Benjamin replied to Evie's accusation. "Evie, your mom and I were very good friends a long time ago. She was the last person I expected to see today and I'm sure the same is true for her as well. It was nice to see her. That's all it is and nothing more. My focus is Luke."

"Okay, Doc, I'm going to talk to my brother now," she said, walking away.

Dr. Benjamin turned and left as well, assessing the amount of disappointment he felt that Evie wanted him to have nothing to do with her mother. The gentle doctor reminded himself that his entire purpose for being there was for Luke, but he had to admit that he felt a familiar sense of excitement from long ago. Excitement that was ever only associated with Rik, his loving nickname for Erika that began a lifetime ago.

***

As Luke's medical team gathered in his room, Mitch and Evie sat on complete opposite sides of the waiting room.

Erika turned to prayer as the medical team worked. It seemed like no time at all before Luke opened his eyes. He looked around and upon seeing Erika, he became agitated and called out, "Ma, Mom, Mom."

Erika jumped to calm him while medial staff watched his vitals on the monitor.

"Shh, shh, shh, Luke. I'm right here. I'm right here, sweetie. Try and stay calm. Just take your time and breathe," she told him.

Dr. Kata ordered a shot of Ativan to control Luke's agitation. He needed to calm down and his doctors needed to prevent any more stress on his body, especially where he was most severely injured.

"Luke, baby," Erika began, "you had an accident."

"That guy's ring. Did he get his ring? It was from his wife. It was their wedding ring," Luke carried on.

"Yes, Luke, he got it. He got it, and he's going to come back in a couple days to thank you," Erika reassured, encouraging her son to try and relax.

Erika was shocked that he hadn't said anything out about baseball as of yet. Once the Ativan got into his system, Luke started to calm down. He was really sleepy now, and it wasn't long before he closed his eyes. His vitals remained stable but natural sleep is exactly what Luke needed. Everyone left the room except for Erika, Dr. Kata, and Dr. Benjamin. Erika sat next to her son, she was happy just watching him sleep as

Dr. Kata and Dr. Benjamin went into an adjacent conference room. She had never been so grateful to see his chest moving up and down on its own. She looked at his abrasions and bruises, and for the first time acknowledged just how lucky Luke was. Erika said a prayer of thanks to God for allowing her to keep her boy with her here. He could have died. Instead, all his organs were spared, and of all people, AJ was there to treat the parts of him that were broken. For a second, Erika allowed to consider that Luke could make a full recovery. Erika was someone who knew to expect the unexpected. Lately, the unexpected had not worked in her favor, but she actually considered that things might be changing.

Erika noticed AJ holding his hand to his mouth, his finger draped over his upper lip. She caught him glancing up at her through the glass with a look of concern on his face. After spending a few more moments with Dr. Kata, they both returned.

Dr. Kata looked at Erika, surprised, "I didn't know you were a doctor, but that's great. It really helps when the parent is better able to understand all of our medical jargon."

"Well, I am, but not really. I don't practice at all anymore."

"Yes, you are!" Dr. Kata contradicted. "Those letters at the end of your name are something you earned and that nobody can take from you," she insisted. Dr. Kata barely finished her sentence before she was paged to the trauma unit and whizzed out the door. As she excused herself, she promised to be back later that afternoon. AJ recommended that they give Evie and Mitch a chance to come back, separately that is, to sit with Luke while they grab a cup of coffee. He needed to explain his reason behind the concerned look on his face. Of course, Mitch was the next to see Luke. Dr. Benjamin quickly introduced himself to Mitch, the two shook hands and Erika and AJ departed. Erika could tell Mitch had no clue who AJ was. He didn't ask, so she didn't offer any more information than she had to. He would probably figure it out in time.

"Alright, Aej," Erika began as they sat down in the hospital cafeteria overlooking a small gazebo that a patron of the hospital donated.

AJ looked at her, and in his very sullen voice he began to explain. "Luke has an infection in his hand or the bones in his hand, more specifically. It's called osteomyelitis and it travels through the blood. As far as we can tell, it hasn't spread to any of the other bones. We've started him on IV antibiotics to prevent it from spreading, but the infection in his hand is extensive."

"Okay, so what does that mean exactly?" Erika asked, trembling.

AJ looked down. "Normally," he said, "an infection such as this isn't much of a concern. We would treat with antibiotics, remove the infected bone if necessary, and the patient would be expected to have a full recovery."

The more in-depth they went into the conversation the more uncomfortable AJ became. He stood up and let his body fall back onto the wall behind where they were conversing. He ran his hands over his face and through his hair. Erika was beginning to understand what her friend was trying to tell her in the gentlest way he knew. Erika interrupted, recognizing that she could take some of the burden from him of having to tell her bad news.

"So, basically what you're telling me is that because of how damaged Luke's hand is, removing the infection is going to difficult?"

"Rik, removing the infection itself isn't the hard part," he told her. "We anticipated having to remove bone in order to reconstruct the hand itself. The problem now is, with this infection, our concern is that he won't have enough viable bone left. In which case, amputating would be Luke's best option."

Erika stared at him wide-eyed and speechless, doing her best to prevent a full panic attack. "Oh," she said. "Um, I, I guess amputating never crossed my mind."

"Rightfully so," he confirmed.

"I need to get back to Luke," she said. "I want to see if he's awake."

AJ followed a few steps behind Erika back to Luke's room. He remembered that when Rik was upset, she needed space. She had to think, and sometimes cry, but then she was able to refocus and do what she needed to do. He hoped the same would apply to this situation, despite the gravity and emotions involved. Luke was still asleep when Erika returned. Evie was sitting at his bedside showing him funny memes.

"He's asleep you know," Erika told to her.

"Oh, I know but they say you should talk to people when they're unconscious," she replied.

AJ laughed and Erika looked at her in disbelief.

"You know he's just sleeping right now, right?" she asked, hoping that Evie really wasn't that clueless. "He came out of his coma early this morning. You knew that."

"Ya know what?" Evie replied. "I think I'm going to go home for a bit. I seriously need to just decompress. My mind is like everywhere." Evie said in defense of her embarrassing brain fart.

"Okay, I guess you're going to have to take my car because I don't want you riding anywhere with Mitch," Erika reminded her.

"You don't have to tell me twice," she replied in haste. "I can't stand that asshole," she declared, hugging her mother before leaving the room.

AJ, still standing beside Erika, was clearly shocked by her comment and somewhat appalled that she would talk that way in front of her mother. Erika looked at him and in support of her daughter commented, "You have no idea how nasty he's been towards her. Just cruel, so don't judge," Erika warned.

AJ wasn't sure of his place. He wanted to help Erika but had the distinct feeling that she wanted him to go. He didn't want to leave. AJ wanted to reach out and touch her shoulder in comfort. He wanted to embrace her. It had been so many years that his feelings didn't make sense. This woman just fell back into his world only hours before and already a flood of feelings returned as if they'd spent every day of the last twenty years together. AJ often thought about Erika and the time he spent with her. She was in most of his favorite memories. AJ felt just as connected and in love with Erika now, instantly, as he had been almost twenty years ago. The kind doctor felt guilty that he was thinking of his own personal wants at a time like this. Erika was so distraught over her son and the condition he was in. There was so much unknown. How could she even feel anything right now, he wondered. There was no doubt in his mind that he, was the furthest thing from hers.

Luke had been sleeping for over four hours before he finally woke up. Surprisingly, he was more lucid than he had been earlier that morning and he was calm. AJ took that as his cue to leave. He told Erika that he would find her later to discuss Luke's upcoming surgery. Surgery was inevitable and Erika understood that. Now she had to tell Luke.

"Hey, sweetie, you awake?" she asked. "Do you remember where you are or what happened?"

"I remember," he said. Luke was very quiet. It was rare that Erika would have to prod him to speak, but she also considered that their conversation was not under normal circumstances. "Is that doctor your friend?" he questioned.

"He is, Luke. He's also an orthopedic surgeon, honey. He's one of the best in the country. It's actually unbelievable that he's here to help you. His name is Dr. Benjamin."

"Was he a patient of yours or something?"

Erika laughed, "No, not quite. Although, I use to question his mental stability," she joked. He and I were in undergraduate and later in med school together," Erika explained.

"Mom," Luke said, the conversation quickly taking a more serious turn, "I'm never going to throw a ball again. I'm never going to LSU. It's all over. You know that, right?"

Erika tried unsuccessfully to soften the tone of the conversation by commenting on how she rarely knows anything that's going on these days but Luke was not having it.

"Mom, stop! Maybe your humor works for you, but I need you to be real. Okay? Can you just be real for a second and talk to me please?" he exclaimed. Erika was speechless.

"Um, uh, yeah, honey, I'm sorry," Erika said, completely caught off guard and trying desperately to hide the lump in her throat. Luke had never snapped at her like that in his life.

"Luke, I guess, um, what I know is that your right hand and your right leg are very badly injured. Your hand is more critical than your leg because you also have an infection and the doctors need to operate and remove parts of bone that are severely infected."

"When?"

"I don't know," she replied. "It's getting late today so I have to talk to the doctor and see if the plan is still to operate today. They could be prepping the OR for you right now and I honestly wouldn't know."

"Well, how about you go find your friend and ask him," Luke said in a sarcastic and snotty tone.

"Luke," Erica said in her newly found confident voice. "I can't even begin to imagine all that is going on in your head. I would take this from you in a minute if I could. I know you are angry and I understand that you need someone to be angry with, so I can be that person for you if you need me to. I want to remind you though that I love you more than life itself. I hope you remember that behind all your anger."

Luke's eyes were welled up with tears in the amount of a small waterfall when he finally blinked. "I know," he said. "Can you please find out when the surgery is?"

"Of course. I will be right back."

"Mom?" he asked. "Just say yes or no, nothing else. Am I going to lose my hand? Is he going to cut it off?"

"I can't tell you yes or no, Luke. Dr. Benjamin won't know what he's dealing with until the surgery is underway, but yes, there's a chance," she confirmed.

"Ma, can you please just go find out now?" he begged.

"Yes. I'm going now. I'm leaving right this second, honey. I will find out everything I can," she assured her son.

His Promise

Erika barely made it out of his room before completely breaking down. A nurse came to help her into a nearby chair. Erika thanked her, but she just needed to talk to AJ. Erika asked the nurse if she could page Dr. Benjamin, but her request fell on deaf ears.

"We just can't go paging doctors each time a family member requests it," she explained. "I know he's consulting with Dr. Langley on another patient just down the hall. I will try to poke my head in and let him know that you would wish to speak with him. Will that work?" she asked.

"Yes, absolutely," Erika affirmed. She sat for a few moments before she saw AJ exit a room at the other end of the hallway. His attention had been fixed on the chart he was reading until the nurse got his attention, causing him to stop and scan the area for Erika. He was halfway through the hallway when he gave Erika a nod to follow him down the opposite hallway. He could see she'd been crying but he resisted any attempt at comforting her. AJ didn't trust himself not to take advantage of the situation to help him get closer to her. Erika came upon him as if he were her savior. Once in a private conference room, Erika fell into his arms, dead weighted and sobbing profusely. She looked up straight into his eyes and his defenses were gone.

"You have to save his hand! Promise me," she plead with him. "Promise me he will have his hand when he comes out of surgery."

AJ knew that he couldn't make her that promise, yet he heard himself say, "Okay, Rik. Okay. I promise. He will keep his hand. I will make it happen. I promise you, sweetie, I promise you."

Surgery was scheduled for 7:00 a.m. the following morning. Erika was relieved to have time to process everything that happened and to have some extra time to update Mitch and Evie. She spent about thirty minutes talking to each of them, explaining what they could expect and the worst-case scenario given Luke's infection. Erika knew the promise she forced AJ into, but realistically she recognized that he might not be able to deliver on that promise. So, she gave each of them every detail as she understood the situation to be. She didn't want to create any false hope.

Erika went back to sit with Luke. His demeanor appeared to be lighter once he knew what to expect and when the surgery would take place. He said that even though he didn't know why, knowing what to expect helped him to feel more in control over his situation. Erika sat by Luke's bed for an hour before a nurse came in and suggested that he sleep, and she injected his IV with his last dose of pain medication for the day.

"Sleep is the best thing you can do, Mr. Luke," she said with a smile. "For your mind and your body, my friend," she continued.

Erika agreed but Luke asked if she would stay for a few more minutes. He just wanted to talk with his mom a bit longer. He had always taken comfort in her presence when he felt sad or insecure. He knew he would need her presence and her support now more than ever. Erika was happy to stay as long as he needed. She held onto his hand as they talked about everything from Evie being ditzy to specific details about the accident. He was calm and she answered every question he had. Baseball, however, was never mentioned this time. Erika was relieved. She sat with him until he fell asleep.

Erika left his room but before she did, she paused to look back at her broken son. She begged God to allow Luke's bones *and* his heart to heal. Erika, of all people, knew the art of suffering and loss, but also knew the art of survival. She would help Luke survive and make things work with whatever "new" he had to work with. "New" could turn out to be great, Erika thought to herself. Somehow, when it came to Luke, she could always find a single ray of sun shining through the window, especially after a door had been closed. Giving up would never be an option. It wasn't for her, and she wouldn't allow it to be for him.

Erika went back and sat in the waiting room for a few minutes as she decided what she should do. She was exhausted and really wanted to go home but it would be an hour by the time Evie could get her and then another hour drive back home. She'd have less than four hours at home before she'd have to leave and come back in time for Luke's surgery. Erika was gross and desperately needed a shower but decided to just sleep in the hospital lobby. She had perfected the art of finding a comfortable position in the awful hospital chairs over the past forty-eight hours. She promised herself that she'd go home once Luke was out of surgery the next day. Erika had just gotten her tired body situated and comfortable when AJ nudged her with a perplexed look on his face.

"I've been looking for you for the past twenty minutes," he said, sounding slightly irritated. "Why are you sleeping here?" he asked. "I thought you'd gone home without saying bye," he continued.

"Oh no!" Erika responded. "I know not to do that," she said with a smile.

"Yeah, yeah, whatever, you bully," he laughed, slightly embarrassed but still smiling.

AJ made a big deal with everyone, not just Erika, about always saying goodbye in case it ended up being the last time they'd ever see each other. It was something he had been taught as a kid, he explained to her years earlier. AJ was teased by everyone, including Erika, about how emotional he would get over saying goodbye. She actually always thought it was endearing what a softy he was.

"There's not enough time to go home and be back before the surgery. I'm just going to sleep here," she told him.

"That's like really dumb," he said, in the less mature, less professional way that she remembered him as. "Plus, you smell so bad you're giving me a migraine," he teased, but with a completely straight face. Erika was just about to implode in reaction to his comment when AJ burst out laughing at the look on her face.

"Asshole!" she yelled so loudly that another person sitting nearby looked up to share a dirty look.

"C'mon, Skuzzy Wuzzy, let's go. My hotel is literally across the street, and I'll treat you to some Walmart attire so you can at least freshen up and get a few hours of sleep. You can take the bed," he assured her.

Erika had to admit that his offer sounded amazing. She craved a hot shower and didn't totally hate the idea of spending time with him either. "Sold," she said and they left.

"Why am I not surprised?" Erika laughed as she approached his candy apple red Porsche.

"My god, woman! It's a rental you ball buster! Damn." AJ exclaimed.

"Oops," Erika said cracking up.

"My real car is a black BMW, sport coupe," he said as if it were a clunker.

Confused, and not wanting to look overly gullible, Erika simply rolled her eyes, a response that wouldn't sell her out that she wasn't sure if he was serious or not. AJ laughed as he slammed her door, got in on his side and they left.

AJ returned from Walmart as Erika was just finishing her shower. He opened the bathroom door, yelled that he wasn't looking and threw a night gown into the bathroom. Once she was out of the bathroom, she saw where he laid out her Walmart attire, impressed that he remembered her style and was dead on for her size. Erika sarcastically thanked him for not making her look like a bag woman.

"Next time, I'll get ya something from The Buckle, but Walmart's the best I can do at midnight," he said, smiling.

Erika's heart melted. She looked up from the text she'd been reading.

"You remember my favorite store?" she asked in a kid like tone.

"Of course, I do. You only owned about twenty pairs of Miss Me jeans," he laughed. "Besides, do you really think I would forget the store that provided me the only opportunity I had to look at your ass *with* your permission? It was my pleasure to tell you which pair of ass bling I liked best," he smirked.

Erika's face dropped, "And there we go," she said. "Moment killed. Gone. Dead. Buried. Thank you, Dr. Benjamin for giving a girl a moment and then ripping it away," Erika said, in the best sad voice she had, pouting.

"I'm kidding," AJ assured, walking over to her and resting his hands on her shoulders. "You'd be surprised at everything I remember about you, Rik," he told her, looking right into her eyes. She just stared back at him, speechless and afraid to blink. She was afraid that if she blinked, the moment would be over, along with a feeling so great, so euphoric, and so beautiful that she couldn't even begin to describe. Erika wanted so badly to kiss him, but then what? She wasn't ready to explore the "then what." She wanted to but wouldn't allow herself.

"Um, I'm beat," she said, quickly moving from him and heading towards the couch. "I'm taking the couch. You're taking the bed," she ordered. "You're operating on the most precious person I have on this earth and the last thing you need is a kinked neck or a sore back."

Before AJ could object, Erika had plopped down onto the couch, wrapped herself in a blanket and buried her face into the corner of the couch. "Goodnight, J of A-ness," she called out. AJ, still standing where he had been with Erika just seconds before, stood unsure of what he should do or say next.

"I have about an hour left of work I need to do before I turn in," he said. "I'll just keep one small light on if that's okay with you," he questioned. He repeated himself again, but Erika was out cold. He chuckled to himself, remembering how she would fall asleep in the first five minutes of every movie they tried watching after 9:00 p.m.

AJ went back to his computer, resuming a chat he'd started earlier with Dr. Altman-Panu, another highly skilled orthopedic surgeon. AJ and Dr. Altman-Panu worked together in Panama and had consulted on the more difficult cases in the States. He knew that Dr. Altman-Panu had treated several cases very similar to Luke's. Their introduction to each other over ten years ago was purely coincidental, but exactly what they both needed. Since that time, the two surgeons became the best of friends, and Dr. Altman-Panu became a priceless mentor to the much younger Dr. Benjamin. After seeing a need, they built a program helping Panamanian natives and, on the other end of the spectrum, Olympic athletes.

In recent years, Dr. Altman-Panu began using AcuPac, as a preferred means of treating some of the most severe bone injuries. Dr. Altman-Panu had been criticized for taking risks and unorthodox forms of treatment. Despite the criticism, Dr. Altman-Panu's success rate has been one of the highest in the country, in Panama, and in Colombia as well. AJ was a more conservative surgeon. Although a wise-guy and former class clown, he never took unnecessary risks. Dr. Altman-Panu thought Luke would be a perfect candidate for AcuPac wherein a white granular product made from the spongy type of bone material in preground sizes is packed into any hole or gap in the bone to fill the defect. AJ had assisted Dr. Altman-Panu with this procedure a handful of times in the past. He was confident in his skill but unsure of the procedure itself. AJ wrapped up his chat with Dr. Altman-Panu who encouraged him one last time to use the procedure, assuring him that it was the best treatment plan and gave Luke the only chance he had of saving his hand, his pitching hand no less.

AJ had given his colleague a bit of his history with Erika, commenting that she was one of his oldest and dearest friends and that her son's condition was severe. AJ's wise colleague knew something was different with this case when he called him asking about the procedure. AJ had expressed nothing but skepticism, and Dr. Altman-Panu thought it would be years before he could convince AJ that the benefit of using AcuPac more than outweighed the potential risks. He knew that AJ liked to play it safe, both in work and in life. Dr. Altman-Panu was curious about this patient and his mother that they would have such an impact on "the young Dr. B.," as he often referred to his friend.

AJ went to turn off the light and stopped where Erika slept. She looked so peaceful nestled in the corner of the couch, her left hand tucked under her chin. AJ bent down and kissed her on the top of her head. The smell of her hair was intoxicating. He sat down next to the couch and rested his head on a small piece of available cushion behind Erika's back. He gently ran his fingertips on a small part of her leg that was exposed. He closed his eyes and fantasized what it would be like to make love to her. He went through every thrust, touch, kiss, and strong embrace. He imagined himself inside her, with his chest pressed up against hers. He wanted to slide his fingers down the side of her breasts, caress her hair, gently pulling it back as he buried his face in her neck, continuing on to taste her lips. He would memorize every part of her beautiful body, her hourglass torso, ticklish to his touch. He couldn't imagine anything more beautiful than making love to her. Moments before he drifted to sleep, still cuddled up behind her, his heart saddened realizing that his fantasy would most likely remain just that, a fantasy. She avoided love, he never stopped working long enough to find love. They led very different lives, and he would soon be leaving the States for several months. Her life was here with her children, and neither of them would abandon those that depended on them so much. Neither would allow themselves to be selfish. Still, for now, she was here and so was he.

Erika was the first to wake, startled to see him next to her. The light remained on all night, and she wondered how he came to sit with her. She slowly turned around. It was her turn now to memorize his beauty. She thought about him back when they were younger and wondered why she never looked at him the way she did now. Was she really that fickle that his height blinded her to all of his amazing qualities? Erika pressed her forehead to his and took a deep breath in.

Their noses touched for a moment and before she knew what she was doing she gently kissed his lips. She wanted more. She kissed his lips again, this time a little harder, causing him to stir ever so slightly. Erika pulled herself back with a palm fist smack to her forehead. What the hell was she thinking? This man was about to operate on her son. He was key to Luke's future and here she was accosting him as he slept after he'd been so kind to her. She felt like he might have feelings for her too, but she'd been mistaken before with men and she was not about to ruin their friendship or their professional patient-doctor relationship. Erika was amazed at how easy it was to be herself around him, just like before. She wished they hadn't lost track of each other all those years ago. She wanted those years back, thinking back to all their great times and countless memories. Erika thought of the person she was then and the person she was now. Nobody would believe they were the same person, but life has a way of making one wise, she thought.

Erika whispered his name quietly in his ear, trying to wake him up. After the third time of calling his name, Erika smiled mischievously and whispered to him, "AJ, I want to ride you hard till you make me cum and I squirt all over your beautiful body. I want to tie you up and lick you from head to toe…." she giggled in a childlike manner as if she was getting away with something. She realized he was getting aroused and the joke was on her. AJ looked up at her with a huge "Chester-cat" like grin on his face.

"Sounds good to me. Sign me up for that ride anytime!" he said almost unable to catch his breath from laughing so hard. He had been awake since the first time she called his name, but he wanted to see how long he could keep her going. He never anticipated she'd whisper what she did. While he was able to keep himself from smiling or laughing at her, his cock obviously had a mind of its own.

"I'm going to kill you! Alexander John Benjamin, you are so dead they're going to have to bury you twice!" she declared.

"I can't help it that you want me. I mean I am irresistible," he baited her. "I usually have to beat chicks off with a stick, but I like you so I'll let you play with my stick and then I'll beat you with it since you like it rough and all," he continued still gasping for air as he laughed. "Listen to you with your kinky tie-me-up shit," he said just as Erika smacked him with her pillow knocking him to the ground.

"You are such a gigantic asshole. I legit hate you," she promised.

"No, you don't," he challenged her.

"It's already 5:30 a.m. We have to go to Luke, so stop being an asshat," Erika demanded, trying to disguise her embarrassment for anger.

AJ came up behind her and turned her around so she would face him. "Tell me you don't hate me," he asked of her in a soft voice.

Erika, pouting refused to look up but admitted, "Of course, I don't hate you. I just feel like an asshole, and I'm just really vulnerable and emotional right now," she said half-crying and half-laughing, while continuing to look down. AJ pulled her to him, lifting her chin with his finger and maneuvering his own body to be on level with hers.

"What is this?" he asked her as wiped a tear from her cheek. "Luke is going to be just great," he reassured her, recognizing that her emotional display was more than just embarrassment. "Remember that promise I made to you?

That Luke will keep his hand?" he asked. Erika nodded. "I'm going to keep that promise, Rik, I will keep my promise," he assured her again. This time, even AJ believed it.

No sooner did AJ finish his sentence, Dr. Altman-Panu called. As much as he hated to kill the moment he and Erika were having, he knew the best thing he could do for both her and Luke was to take that phone call. Erika cleaned up where she had laid for her few hours of rest. While AJ talked, referencing his laptop several times, then turning away to jot down a couple of notes, Erika pulled herself away from her trance and headed to the bathroom to get dressed. Today was a life-changing day for Luke and she needed to have her head on straight. Erika noticed one of AJ's shirts laying across the towel bar. She picked it up and held it to her face. She tucked it under her chin momentarily and took in a deep breath where she was able to capture his scent to memory. Erika returned the shirt to where AJ had it and finished freshening up. AJ was done with his call by the time she came out of the bathroom. She quickly turned away after she interrupted him changing shirts.

"It's okay, Rik. I'm not naked," he laughed. "I can be though, if you wanted to tie me up like you mentioned earlier," he teased again, thinking back to all the times he'd purposely antagonize her to get a reaction.

Exasperated, Erika held her hand up in front of her face. "Don't even," she warned him.

AJ finished changing shirts and Erika continued to look away.

"It's a good thing you didn't come out a second earlier, I had my pants off, you probably would have jumped out the window," he said continuing to antagonize her.

"Ha-ha, jackass," she muttered to herself. "Ready?" she asked, noting the time.

"I am," he said confidently, staring at her with a look that told her "I got this."

Erika smiled and they left for the hospital.

As they drove to the hospital, they discussed the details of the surgery and AJ explained what would happen that morning.

"I conferred with another one of my colleagues," he began. "There's a procedure that he uses frequently and swears by it. I have to admit, it works. I am usually more conservative, but I trust him and he's right. Luke is the type of patient this procedure is designed for, and I'm going to use it. I called the hospital and arranged for what I would need. Everything will be ready to go when we get there," AJ explained. He looked over and saw Erika smiling, causing him to smile in turn. He patted her hand, "So, no more tears and no more beating my ass with a pillow either. Damn, that hurt, Little Miss Tiny But Mighty."

Erika's smile widened. AJ couldn't help but keep one eye on her and the other on the road.

As they parked, Erika turned to him and with her guard down and her voice cracking as she spoke, she said, "Thank you for everything, AJ. I mean it. I don't know how or why we drifted apart all those years ago, but that's not happening again."

He smiled back at her, elated. "I would do anything for you, Rik," he said, and she believed that he would.

A Helping Hand

Erika and AJ walked in the hospital together chatting and headed to Luke's room. Erika wondered where Mitch was, but she'd given him all of the information so aside from shooting him a text, she wasn't going to worry. AJ stopped at the nurses' station and Erika stepped aside to talk to Mitch who'd called her in response to her text. AJ was met with curious smirks and assumptions, as they watched he and Erika walk in together, more like a couple than a doctor with the mother of a patient.

"Really?" he said to the nurses sitting closest to him, with the biggest grin. "This isn't even my own hospital. and I have the nurse-cult giving me crap already," he laughed. "Do you guys have like your own closed group Facebook page of nurses or something where you post about the scandalous docs in your hospital?" he joked. "I bet if I look hard enough, I will find a post or two about my manhood and some other weird voodoo things you crazy women do to guys like me," he teased.

Deidre, the head nurse, known for her quick wit, replied, "Doc," she said, gesturing for him to come closer to her. "That one is crazy about you," she said, pointing to Erika, "and I can just tell that she'd like to try out your manhood, so you do what you gotta do, and we'll let you read our Facebook posts for advice," she laughed.

"Thank you, Deidre. Ms. Doss is a friend of mine from medical school," he assured her.

"I'm sure she is, Dr. B.," Deidre replied, patting him on the shoulder and with a look on her face that told AJ he wasn't filing anyone. "We appreciate you here, Dr. B. We love working with you. Wish you were here all the time, but we'll take what we can get," she said, changing the topic, returning to a level of appropriateness.

"Thank you, Deidre," AJ repeated with an eye roll. He enjoyed the few times he'd consulted in Ann Arbor and wished he'd have known that Erika was so close all times, but there was no point in dwelling about that now. It would be a very long time before he'd be returning once Luke and his one other patient were stable. Erika caught up with him and they continued to Luke's room.

Deidre called out, "Oh, and Dr. B.," she said, "you'll have to tell me about your handsome little friend later on. I've been single a long time, and I wouldn't mind getting to know him," she smiled, somewhat jokingly, yet still serious.

"What? Who?" he asked, just before he heard a familiar voice.

AJ and Erika walked into Luke's room to see Evie sitting on the corner of his bed and next to them stood Dr. Altman-Panu. Luke was smiling. He looked good and he was laughing with his sister and the kind doctor.

"Hey, Mom. Hey Dr. Benjamin," Luke said enthusiastically.

Evie was less enthusiastic to see her mother walk in with AJ. She thought about embarrassing her mother by asking where she was all night, but she didn't want to do that to Luke. AJ went over to his friend and colleague, giving him a half man-hug, half handshake.

Shocked, AJ asked, "What are you doing here? You're completely crazy!"

Dr. Altman-Panu responded, talking directly to Luke, "Dr. Benjamin is the best, but I'm better," he joked.

Returning his attention back to AJ and in his more sincere and professional regard, he informed them of his intent. "I'm here to support a very good doctor and a very good friend," adding, "if you don't mind, that is."

"Erika, you remember how I was telling you about my colleague and our discussion about Luke's procedure?" he began.

"I like how it sounds, Mom," Luke interrupted. "He thinks it's the best and I have a feeling it will work. It's the only chance I have at playing ball again," he said.

Erika felt dizzy and both doctors shared a similar look, concerned that Luke's hope in returning to baseball might be unrealistic.

AJ redirected his attention back to Erika and finished the introduction.

"Erika Doss, meet Dr. Peta Altman-Panu or Dr. Pap as we like to call him."

"Pleasure, ma'am. You have a beautiful family, and AJ was right, you're very beautiful yourself," Dr. Pap commented.

Evie rolled her eyes in disgust.

"Thank you," Erika responded, embarrassed but smiling. She was still a bit confused at everything but focused on Evie and wondered what was behind her attitude all of a sudden. On the other hand, she was happy to see the improvement in Luke's attitude and demeanor.

"So, you'll be working with AJ this morning?" she asked. Catching the confused look on his face, AJ reminded Dr. Pap that he'd known Erika long ago, back when he went by a less professional sounding name.

"That's right," Dr. Pap responded. Directing his attention back to Erika, he affirmed that he would be operating on Luke alongside Dr. Benjamin, or AJ, as she referred to him.

Both surgeons departed and went to scrub in while transport was called to take Luke to pre-Op.

Evie kissed her brother, reminded him how much she loved him and left. She passed Mitch in the hallway but refused to acknowledge his existence.

"Hello, Evie," Mitch said, trying to break the ice, unsuccessfully.

She heard him but didn't even flinch in response to his gesture. Instead she thought, "Go to hell," managing to keep the words from flying off her lips.

Before leaving, Erika reassured her son and was pleased by his continued optimism. Luke even told his mother he loved her before she had the opportunity to say it first. In keeping with the events over the past few days, Erika was shocked at what Luke said next.

"Your friend is pretty cool, Mom. They both are. I can't even imagine what it would be like to live near and work in a tribe in Panama. It's kinda weird that the people there are accepting of Western medicine, but I guess they are, and those docs are pretty great people for helping all those kids. I think they pay for a lot of it themselves too," he added.

"Wait, what?" Erika for about the hundredth time over the past forty-eight hours.

Luke didn't have the chance to clear up his mother's bewilderment. Mitch, and a few seconds later, Ump Ted, walked into Luke's room. They only had moments to wish him well.

Luke thanked the Ump Ted for coming, who in turn apologized for not having gotten there sooner. He thanked Luke for his kindness of heart and told him what a great young man he was for saving the old man's treasure. Luke accepted a hug from the grateful umpire. Hoping for a second to talk his dad, as they wheeled him out, Luke and Ump Ted agreed that he'd come back the next day.

Mitch was disappointed he hadn't gotten a chance to really converse with Luke but was happy to have exchanged an "I love you" before the elevator doors closed. Mitch and Erika stood hand in hand as their son went off to surgery. Now all they could do was wait and pray.

Mitch went on his way to run some errands and Erika found her place in the lobby. Evie sat across from her but refused to look at her.

"So, how was your night, *Erika*?" she said in a sarcastically.

"It was fine, *Evelyn Jean*. How was yours?" she responded, letting Evie know that she was not about to be bullied by her daughter.

"So, did you guys get to relive your college years?" Evie bated.

"Evie, if you have something to say, then let's step outside, and I will be happy to address answer your innuendos,"

Erika said. "I have too much respect for the other people sitting in this room to engage in your passive aggressive temper-tantrum," she continued.

"Fine!" Evie responded, violently pushing her chair back from under her.

The two highly agitated females walked outside until they found a bench in which to continue their banter. Erika was able to compose herself back to something resembling a mother and placed her frustration with her misinformed daughter aside.

"Evie, what is wrong? Why are you so angry with me?"

"Did you sleep with him?" Evie asked.

"Um, not that it's any of your business, but no, I didn't."

"You want to," she challenged.

"Evie," Erika explained, "Luke wanted me to stay with him last night. I was here until at least 11:30 p.m., if not later. I was tired. I planned to call you for a ride home, but it wasn't worth it since I needed to be back here by 6:00 a.m. I was going to sleep in the lobby, but AJ offered for me to stay at his hotel and I accepted his offer. He worked most of the night. I took a shower and crashed on the couch. What is your problem with AJ anyway?" Erika asked her.

"Well, whatever," Evie responded, still with an attitude. "I already told him that your vagina was Fort Knox anyway and not to even think about it."

"You said what?" Erika exclaimed. "How dare you talk to another adult about me in such a way. Have you lost your mind? What if I embarrassed you like that?" Erika demanded.

"I'm sorry, Mom. I'm sorry." Evie yelled.

"Oh, at least I'm your mother again and not Just 'Erika' to you," Erika jabbed, not able to help herself.

"Mom! Stop it, please! For as long as I've known you, you've told me how life is a bitch and how guys just make everything worse. Now, when Luke is hurt, you're all gaga for his doc. We need you, Mom. Luke and me, we need you. I'm sorry, Mom. I know it's not fair, but we need you. Mitch hates and blames me for Luke. If that doc takes you away, what do I have left?" Evie explained, now crying. "Like, my real mom is dead but it's easier when someone dies because you can't do anything about it. It's worse when the person you need and love is so close, but no matter what you try, you can't reach them."

Now softened and saddened by Evie's speech, Erika reassured her that she would never just stop being their mom. "Eves," she began, "I'm your mother and Luke's mother. Without the two of you, I am nothing. My heart would be so empty that it would just stop beating," she assured her. "This is such a crazy life, and I am not sure of anything except for the fact that death would be the only thing to keep me from loving and taking care of you. Even then, I would spend my days in Heaven watching over the two of you, guiding you from above. You'd feel a bump on the head if you were being stupid or a breeze across your cheek to tell you how proud I am of you when you're being great," Erika continued. "Eves, look at me," she said. "I know life has been unkind to you. I know how badly you've been hurt, and I know how your heart has suffered. I assure you, sweetie, your heart and your love is one of my most treasured gifts, and I would never give up my most valued treasure for anything or anyone," Erika promised her.

Erika understood that even more than she, Evie had been through the emotional ringer these past few days. Not only did she see her brother, her dearest friend, crushed by a truck, but someone she trusted revealed his disdain for her. Now she saw her mother acting differently than ever before combined with already having lost one mother. Erika was sympathetic to Evie's fear.

"I'm sorry, Mom. I'm sorry," Evie said, still crying. "I'll apologize to Dr. Benjamin for what I said," Evie offered.

"You know what, kiddo, I don't think that's necessary," Erika said, not wanting to cause any more embarrassment or discomfort to her already fragile daughter. "He's fine," Erika assured.

The mother and daughter walked, arms linked, to the hospital cafeteria. They both needed food and to be in a slightly different environment for a while. It had been two hours since Luke's surgery began. They knew to expect it to last at least seven to eight hours, but remaining patient was no easy feat. Erika snorted her coffee in response to Evie's next random comment.

"I'd fuck him," she said. "Dr. B, I mean. He's hot, but you already know that, don't you, Mama Bear?" Evie found great amusement in her comment as she waited a response from her mother. "Oh, here comes the look," Evie declared.

"I have no looks to give, Evie. Sorry to disappoint you," Erika stated, straight faced as if she really believed Evie's impression to be false. "Dr. Benjamin and I have been friends for a very, very long time. That is it, period." Erika declared.

"Okay, okay," Evie conceded, not wanting to piss her mom off any more than she already had. "I guess it doesn't really matter anyway," Evie asserted. "If you're not going to leave me and Luke, you're not going to have anything more than a good fuck every once in a while with a guy who lives in Panama the majority of the year," Evie said.

"What is up with your obsession with 'F-ing,' Evie? Really? Can we limit the amount of times you use the 'F word' in the same hour, please?" Erika asked, now annoyed at Evie and upset at the information she just learned.

AJ wouldn't be around much longer, and that's why Evie was so worried about losing her. Things made sense now and with that, Erika excused herself and headed to the restroom. Her two-minute tour of the cafeteria, while trying to find the bathroom was a blur. It was then that she realized she really didn't know anything about AJ anymore. She knew his personality but nothing about his life. She had been looking at him as if they were still college kids where she'd be able to plop down on the couch next to him whenever she wanted. That was far from the case. Erika wondered if he had children or if he had ever married. Erika couldn't believe that she hadn't taken the time to ask him any of these questions. Yet, her children knew that he lived in Panama, of all places. What the hell is in Panama, she wondered. Then she recalled that Luke had mentioned something about a tribe and being accepting of Western medicine. "Oh my God," Erika said aloud, still in the bathroom stall. *AJ must help kids that live in tribal communities*, she thought to herself, *and Dr. Peta Altman-Panu was his partner.*

Erika and Evie spent the next several hours going in between the cafeteria, the chapel, and the main surgical waiting room.

"You okay?" Evie asked her.

"I mean, yeah, as good as I'm going to be considering the circumstances," Erika replied.

"And what circumstances might you be referring to, Mama Bear?" Evie asked, while purposefully bumping Erika's leg to show that she was serious but also not trying to offend her.

"Luuukkkee," Erika stressed, as she tried to avoid eye contact with Evie. Evie was the only one who could read her like a book, but her mind was in too much of a cluster to try and explain what she was feeling to Evie, especially when she didn't know herself.

"Mom," Evie began, gently smirking. "You went to the bathroom as soon as I mentioned that Dr. Benjamin lived in Panama. You passed me three different times trying to find the bathroom that was fifty feet in front of you. You were totally lost in thought, and you bumped into the condiment station twice," she said laughing her ass off by this time.

Erika looked at her wide-eyed in disbelief.

"It doesn't take another orthopedic surgeon to tell me that you're in to this one," Evie concluded, still laughing at her mother. Erika was trying so hard not to give herself up that she was literally holding her breath until she no longer could. The two of them rolled laughing hysterically, stopping only to make sure they weren't offending anyone nearby.

"I bumped into the condiment station?" Erika asked. She had no recollection of that whatsoever.

"Yep! Twice," Evie confirmed.

"Wow," Erika replied.

When they finally stopped laughing, Evie returned to her original question. "You okay?" Evie repeated.

Erika stopped to think for a minute before replying. "I mean, yeah. I guess I'm disappointed that he'll be leaving soon. He was my friend back then and he's my friend now. I think I was shocked that there is so little that I really know about him anymore. For whatever reason, that really bothers me, and I have no idea why," she explained.

To her surprise, Evie understood why. She looked at her mom ever so sincerely and said, "I think it bothers you that there could be something else in his life that is more important to him than you, and you have no way of knowing what or who that could be. You don't even know what it is that you have no control over."

Apparently, Evie had a good read on AJ, too, surprisingly. Erika didn't even get a chance to respond to Evie's astute insight before they saw the surgeons heading down the hallway towards them, now almost nine hours later from when they first began.

Erika tried to read AJ's face as he walked, but he was still engrossed in discussion with Dr. Pap. When they came upon where Erika and Evie stood, AJ looked up and gave her the biggest smile she had ever seen from him. Erika exhaled. AJ grabbed her and held her close to him.

He kissed her on the head, and with his cheek still resting on the top of her head, he reported that Luke was doing great. Once AJ finally released her, the two surgeons walked them into a conference room and quickly explained what they had done to repair and re-set Luke's leg before moving on to discuss his hand.

"His hand was a challenge," AJ admitted. We spent the majority of our time on the hand, but we were able to get all of the infected bone out and we filled areas of the hand with the spongy bone material that we told you about and explained how it's used," he continued. "Most importantly, we were able to save his hand!"

Once she processed what the handsome surgeon just said, Erika buried her head in her hands and sobbed. Evie soon joined her in tears of relief and joy. AJ smiled to himself, feeling relieved and so very grateful to the "surgeon gods" that he was able to keep his promise.

Dr. Pap was the first to kill the moment by acknowledging the extensive amount of physical therapy and rehabilitation Luke would require. Erika had kept PT in the back of her mind, but she wasn't prepared for the reality of it. Luke needed four to six hours of rehab, five to six days a week for an unspecified period of time.

Evie beat Erika to the question that had been on their minds all day.

"What are the chances that Luke could play college ball next year or even the year after that?" she asked, feeling hopeful.

Erika knew the answer to that question as soon as it left Evie's lips. She could feel AJ's discomfort in having to answer.

"He won't be able to, will he?" Erika interjected, waiting to hear his response.

"No, Rik. I don't think so," he said apologetically.

Dr. Pap took over trying to explain about elasticity and range of motion, but Erika heard nothing else after that. Evie, too, seemed equally distracted after learning of Luke's unfortunate fate. Erika tried to remain as enthusiastic as she was upon first learning that they were able to save Luke's hand. Truthfully, she was heartbroken for her son's loss, but the important thing was that the docs were able to save his hand. As long as he still had his hand, anything was possible. Erika hugged both doctors and they headed back to the recovery room. Erika and Evie headed to Luke's hospital room to wait for his return. Erika called Mitch in the meantime, who said he'd be over shortly to see their son. He, too, was elated at the news that the doctors were able to save Luke's hand. Erika and Evie sat speechless until Luke retuned.

Expect the Unexpected

Luke returned heavily sedated and AJ told them not to expect too much coherent conversation from him for the rest of the day. Erika tried to figure out the plan for the night. Evie asked if she could have a friend pick her up since Luke was still out of it and she still wanted nothing to do with being around Mitch. The surgeons were done for the day and were also making plans to head out.

"I can drive you home, Rik. I mean, as long as you don't care, let her take the car." AJ suggested. Coincidentally, Dr. Pap stuck his head in Luke's room and offered to take everyone to dinner while Luke slept. Erika agreed to let Evie take the car while she, AJ, and Dr. Pap went to dinner. Mitch was glad too. He hadn't had much alone time with Luke and even if he was asleep, Mitch felt better just being near to him.

Erika walked Evie to the car and they finally talked about Luke not being able to play baseball.

"How do you think he's going to take it?" Evie inquired.

"Not well," Erika confessed. "Not well at all," she repeated.

"What are we going to do?"

"I don't know. I honestly don't know. We'll be there for him," she said, feeling helpless. "That's all we can do."

"Be safe," Erika directed Evie. "Have fun and try to keep your mind off of all this sad stuff," she said.

"I will."

As Evie pulled out of her parking space, she rolled her window down, "Hey, Mom," she called out. "Just enjoy him while he's here," she advised her mother, in reference to AJ. "Just say 'fuck it' and live in the here and now," Evie instructed.

"There's that word again! Evelyn Jean, for the second time, please remove that word from your vocabulary!"

Evie thought for a moment, and then replied, "Probably not. I'm sorry, Mom, it's one of my favorite words. I like the forcefulness of the strong consonant sounds. And," she continued, "maybe if you actually *do* that word to him, you'll come to like the word too!" Evie laughed, feeling so proud of herself and her deranged sense of humor.

"There's something seriously wrong with you, child," Erika told her, only half-jokingly. "My dear, how about you just worry about you?" Erika suggested, laughing and rolling her eyes as Evie drove off.

Erika walked back in the hospital just to walk back out moments later with AJ and Dr. Pap. Erika and AJ drove separately since Dr. Pap was heading to the airport after dinner. Erika was surprised that Dr. Pap preferred to eat at a dive country bar down river over a more elegant restaurant in downtown Ann Arbor, and her face showed it. AJ laughed at Erika's reaction.

"The more you get to know him, you'll find that Pap's full of surprises," AJ informed her. "You never know what you're going to get with him, like randomly showing up in hospitals to assist with surgery without any warning or prior clearance from the hospital," AJ laughed, continued to shake his head.

Without thinking, Erika said what she had been thinking. "He's not the only one full of surprises," she commented, looking away from him.

AJ stopped in his tracks, reaching out for Erika's arm as they reached AJ's cherry apple rental Porsche. "What's wrong?" he asked, concerned. "You've been distant but I assumed it was because of Luke. Are you mad me because of Luke's hand?" he asked her in a serious tone. "Rik, I did everything I could do…"

"Of course not," Erika interrupted him. "I know you did and I'm so grateful. I don't even want to think of what could have been had you not been here."

"Then what is it?" AJ asked for the second time.

As Erika paused to respond, Dr. Pap pulled up next to them.

"C'mon, I'm following you," he said.

"Are you sure you want to go to Diamondback?" AJ asked again, hoping his answer would be "no."

"Absolutely!" he said. "It's right next to the airport. I want to drink beer and hit on trashy women," he said, trying to go for the shock factor. "Alex, there's something wrong with your friend's face," he joked, bringing attention to the look of dismay on Erika's face. "Her face gets all squishy every time I say something. She thinks I'm coo-coo," Dr. Pap said, feeling confident of his accurate summation regarding her opinion of him.

Laughing, Erika and AJ both looked at him and as if previously rehearsed, responded "YES!" simultaneously.

"You guys are boring! Let's go!" he said, honking his horn as motivation for them to get moving.

AJ and Erika got in the car and led the way to Dr. Pap's country dive bar.

"This should be an adventure," he said, rolling his eyes in reference to his eccentric friend.

Erika hoped she could dodge the bullet of revisiting the conversation they were having moments before Dr. Pap's interruption in the parking garage, but she wasn't that lucky. She could feel him staring at her as he drove.

"Well," he said. "What's wrong?"

"I was just surprised to hear you live in Panama. I thought your home base was in Colorado," she said.

Now he had her cornered. She had let on that she had feelings for him, otherwise his location wouldn't matter.

"Actually," he said, "Colorado is my home base but yes, I do live in Panama about nine months of the year. I'm sorry I didn't tell you," he said. "I guess I didn't want to have that conversation with you," he admitted.

"Don't be sorry," Erika replied. "It's not like you owe me anything," she said.

"Please don't do that."

"Do what?"

Erika knew exactly what he meant. She was being passive-aggressive and he knew her well enough to call her out.

"Obviously, you don't want me to leave, but why? I know why I didn't want to have this conversation with you," he said. "It's because I don't want to leave you," he told her, as a matter of fact. "Why don't you want me to leave? Is it because you want me here for Luke? Or do you want me here for you?" he asked, pressuring her for a response.

Bam! She was saved by coo-coo Dr. Pap once again. He was ready to go the minute he pulled in behind them. Dr. Pap jumped out his car and opened AJ's car door.

"Let's go!" he demanded.

"This conversation isn't done," AJ vowed, touching her hand, while looking right into her eyes without even flinching.

Dr. Pap looked like a kid at Christmas, enjoying the dive bar atmosphere. He flirted with the waitresses at the bar, enjoying a handful of stale peanuts before joining Erika and AJ at their table.

"Not that I expect anyone to take me out for dinner, but nasty bar food and stale peanuts, wasn't what I had in mind, especially after not eating anything but hospital cafeteria food for the past several days," Erika joked. In an effort to evade AJ's questions, she urged Dr. Pap to tell her all about Panama and the work they do there. Erika figured she could get all the information she wanted from the chatty, overzealous Dr. Pap versus giving herself away even further by directing her questions to AJ.

"Oh my God, it's fantastic!" Dr. Pap exclaimed, referring to the compound he and AJ built and invested in over the past ten years. "It's just outside the Embera Village, deep in the rainforest," he explained. "We treat nearby tribal children from different villages in Panama and Colombia. We always initially consult in their tribe, and then transport them to our compound, but depending on the case, especially for kids, we may stay in their village and treat the child there for as long as necessary. Some cases are too severe to be transported," he explained in great detail. "It's amazing, but the tribes have really taken to us. They trust us now," he said proudly.

AJ sat with his back against the wall. He couldn't imagine what Erika was thinking, listening to Dr. Pap ramble on.

"Oh, yeah, and now we get some of the injured Olympians too," Dr. Pap blurted.

AJ covered his eyes with his hand, leaving a crack in between his fingers so he could sneak a look at Erika's expression.

"Olympians?" she asked. "You treat tribal communities in Panama and Colombia, and you treat Olympians too?" she repeated, slightly laughing at how bizarre that sounded. "Do you mind if I ask how in the world you ended up with that combination?" she had to ask.

"Well, we have Alex to thank for that," Dr. Pap replied.

"Of course, you do. Why not?" she said looking at AJ, shaking her head in utter amazement.

Reluctantly, AJ uncovered his face to better explain what Dr. Pap was yammering about.

"Do you remember my way younger sister, Carrie?" he asked Erika.

"Oh yeah, vaguely, but yes," she replied.

"Well, she was on the 2016 Olympic team in Rio," he began. "About two months before the Summer Games, she fractured her spine. Repairing the spine was the easy part. Rehab was the challenge, especially since we only had two months to work with," he explained. "So, she stayed with me in Panama and we worked her, and worked her, and worked her. I felt like I was abusing my little sister, but it was what she wanted, and her hard work paid off. Carrie placed on the uneven bars, but don't ask me if it was silver or bronze or whatever. I forget that stuff," he said, as if it were normal to forget which medal your little sister won—in the Olympics!

"Wow," Erika responded, after picking her jaw up off the ground.

"So, anyway," Dr. Pap but in, "Every injured Olympian comes to us now, but we only take them if we can. The tribal communities are our priority," he insisted. "Enough of this talk-talk. I'm going to get my line dance on," Dr. Pap declared, beer in hand.

"That is one weird dude," Erica said aloud, but meant for just herself. "Yeah, I don't even know what to say," she began, but before she could finish, Dr. Pap whisked her onto the dance floor. Erika shot AJ a look that told him to get his ass up there. She had to admit that it was hysterical watching Dr. Pap and AJ trying to keep up with the line dance. They looked absolutely ridiculous and Erika could hardly contain her laughter. AJ started chucking peanuts at her so she'd stop laughing at him. She had to admit to herself that she hadn't had this much fun in a very long time.

The mood quickly turned from a fast-paced line dance to a slow country love song. Erika tried to make her way back to their table, but AJ had other ideas. He pulled her near and she recognized the song as one of her favorite country songs, John Michael Montgomery's *Hold on to Me,* and that's exactly what she did. Erika held onto AJ, secretly thankful to Dr. Pap for forcing them to this dive bar. Neither of them spoke a word as they slow-danced, except to point out that Dr. Pap had kidnapped an unsuspecting waitress and whisked her onto the dance floor. They held each other, Erika holding tightly to the back of AJ's neck, and he, pressing his hand on her back, moving her even closer to him. Lost in each other, it took a moment for Erika to notice that the song had changed. When she finally recognized the new song as Toby Keith's, *You Shouldn't Kiss Me Like This*, she knew she was in trouble.

AJ whispered in her ear, "Why don't you want me to leave, Rik?" he asked her, waiting to hear the answer he was hoping for. "Do you want me to stay for Luke or do you want me to be close to you?"

Erika closed her eyes for a moment and then looked up at AJ, who was patiently awaiting her response. Erika opened her mouth to speak, but instead she pulled his face to hers and kissed him like she'd never kissed anyone before. His mouth was warm, and he felt so soft on her lips. She couldn't say what happened after that or if she ever did tell him that she wanted him to stay for her. She just clung to him, dancing, and praying the song would never end so she wouldn't have to let go. Dr. Pap tapped AJ on the shoulder and quickly waved goodbye as he headed out to catch his flight. When they finally returned to their table, AJ sat across from her staring and smiling at her.

"What?" Erika asked, sheepishly.

"Erika James," he said baiting her, "you like me."

"Stop!" she demanded, flicking the rest of Dr. Pap's popcorn at him.

"Come here," he told her, as he pulled her up and onto his lap.

He wrapped his arms around her waist, locked her hands with his, smelled her hair, and kissed the back her neck. AJ was the happiest he'd ever been. It had taken twenty years, but he was finally holding his "Rik," and she was holding him back.

Finally Their Time

The next few weeks with AJ were the best Erika had ever had. She was in love and it started with a single kiss. Dr. Pap would later try to take credit for their relationship, being the one who had insisted on the dive bar versus a more reputable establishment, but Erika and AJ knew better. It would have been a matter of time. Despite his status of being a self-proclaimed workaholic, and she, having sworn off men, their love began twenty years ago whether they knew it or not and neither of them would be able to resist a second chance.

Erika and AJ left the bar that night, but she didn't go home. Erika felt whole, and for the first time ever, she felt happiness deep in her soul. She spent the majority of the car ride home with the top down, sitting on AJ's lap as he drove, kissing his face, touching him. She acted as if she were back in college, and not a mother of two with the weight of the world on her shoulders. She felt the wind blowing in her hair and the warmth of the summer night on her skin. AJ carried Erika into his hotel room, her legs wrapped around his waist, her hands embedded in his hair.

A million thoughts ran through AJ's mind as he embraced his Rik. She was more beautiful at forty than back when they were kids. He remembered all the times he had thought about her, especially when he was lonely. He'd love to lay on the beach, the sounds of the ocean crashing around him, and he'd think of her. He thought about her intoxicating laugh and her green eyes that stared off into the distance when she deep in thought, or if she were happy, how the whole world knew, but if she were sad, only he would know. His thoughts wandered to the weird looks she'd give him when he was being a "dumb guy," and how she'd cry at sad movies with children and dogs. He remembered how she'd jump on his back unexpectedly and they'd both tumble forward. AJ spent so many years of his life dedicated to medicine and helping others that Erika consumed the majority of the only memories he had of the times he spent being happy himself. He wondered if he purposely submerged his life into others so he wouldn't have to replace her in his heart or fail at relationships because nobody could ever take her place in his heart. Up until now, Erika had never looked at him as he did her, but he was happy just to have her next to him.

Now, here she was, holding onto him, and he finally had what he'd waited so long for.

AJ laid Erika on his bed. He felt her face, and she held his hand to her lips. She kissed the hands that had worked so hard to help her son. He pulled off the shirt he had bought for her the night before and kissed her neck, her chest, down to her stomach, her bra straps falling off of her shoulders. She lunged forward and wrapped his face in her chest, reaching behind him to pull off his shirt, revealing his tan sculpted body. She ran her fingers across his back, outlining his shoulders, and following them as they moved to touch her. His hands ran across her breasts and down the sides of her torso, sending a tingle, and then a shiver bursting through her body. Her hands went across his thighs, moving upward. She felt him against her, and she wanted him inside her. He refused to let her take over, continuing to please her. AJ removed her panties, and she felt his warm mouth brush up against her labia. He had the softest lips, causing another burst of heaven to erupt throughout her body. His fingers caressed the inside of her thighs, soon to join where his lips were, warmly invited the by way of her clitoris. She felt a pool of moisture as he kissed her deeper and longer, the lips of her most sensitive body spot tightening, as proof of the passion they shared. AJ moved upward again, and his lips found their natural place on hers, his hands outlining the circles of her hardened nipples, yelling for him to taste them. Erika found it hard to control the pleasure she felt. He followed the path of her arms, pulling them over her head, their fingers locked, and his entire body pressed against hers. Erika finally won the battle, weakening his grip and rolling him over to show her dominance.

AJ grabbed her face.

"Erika," he said, looking through her eyes.

She smiled back at him as if to return what he was telling her with his heart. No words were necessary. She reached behind her to relocate her bra that had been tossed aside. She sat up, each leg hovering over one side of his body and she held up her bra. Her mischievous smile returned, along with a childish giggle showing how proud she was of what she was about to do. Erika unhooked her bra straps and one by one, she tied his wrists behind him. AJ had to laugh at her resourcefulness. She got her wish to tie him up, and only a day after she whispered the idea out into the universe. AJ closed his eyes. She kissed his lips, buried her head in his neck, and paused to whisper, "AJ, you have my heart," she said, quickly putting her finger to his mouth, not allowing hm to speak. She wanted him to know she'd fallen but that was the only way she could tell him, and she hoped he felt it in her touch. Powerless, AJ laid back, and felt pleasure soar through his body. It was his heart though that was exploding. He had Erika's heart. He was certain that his life was about to change. No matter what, his life had to include her. He had to find a way, he thought. Just as the thought of she and Luke coming with him to Panama entered his mind, he was distracted by her warm mouth wrapped around his cock. Her tongue, caressing the tip of his penis and her hands stroking him with her gentle glide. He felt pressure building inside of him and he had to take her.

AJ worked his hands out of her capture, rolling her back over, he on top of her and back in control. He lifted himself above her, outlining his muscular triceps.

"Rik, you've always had my heart," he said. "I've loved you forever, every day, even when you were gone from my life, you were never gone from my heart," AJ confessed.

Speechless, Erika knew she would never forget this moment. She closed her eyes and a tear fell down her cheek, and she felt him inside her for the first time. She let out a sigh of passion and wrapped him in her arms. They made love, all the while holding onto each other, forehead to forehead, exchanging a passionate look with a long deep kiss. They made love like that for hours, falling asleep in each other's safe embrace, AJ with his head buried in her neck, his lips pressing against her shoulder and Erika with her arms wrapped tightly around his, pressed firmly against her heart. They thought the night would never end.

Erika woke up alone. Panicked, she called out for AJ before realizing the note he left for her on his pillow. It read, "In the shower, my love. Join me?" Excited, Erika smiled, jumped out of bed, and ran to the shower. She opened the shower door, pausing to stare at the beautiful man in front of her. AJ said nothing. He simply smiled, held out his hand, and brought her near to him. She giggled as he grabbed her face pulling it in to his. The water ran down their bodies as they stayed lost in each other's kiss, aware of only each other.

They made love again, pausing to tease one another, laughing together. AJ teased her that he'd been there the whole time waiting just for her while she passed him up for every other loser she dated. Erika got the last word.

"Aej, I'm sorry. I know it must have been hard on you watching me date those other guys but I had no other choice. You were too short, and I couldn't see you there standing in line waiting for me when everyone five feet seven or taller towered you!" She jabbed.

"Oh, I see how it is," he said, picking her up, her legs returning to their rightful place, wrapped around his body. They laughed, playfully attacked each other, and took time to pause from their ruckus to enjoy a quiet moment with their noses pressed together, kissing one another softly. AJ carried her out of the shower and back to the bed. He sat up next to her and traced a heart in the palm of her hand.

"Hold onto it for me," he told her.

Erika cupped her hand and held it against her heart. He pushed her hair back away from her face and whispered in her ear, "This is where it starts, Rik. This is where we start, you and me forever. You'll never be lonely, and you'll never feel broken again. I'll always want only you."

Crying, still unable to speak to say the actual words, Erika lipped, "I love you."

He kissed her one final time before allowing their day to start.

Erika Exposed

The couple drove to the hospital together, as they had yesterday, but so much was different now. In one day, two lives changed and two hearts had fallen. It was all they could do to hide their glow as they entered Luke's room. Evie was sitting on the corner of her brother's bed taking selfies with him and making fun of Instagram posts. Erika was thrilled to see her children like this.

"Luke!" Erika said. "How are you? How do you feel? Oh my God, you're awake and have some life in you!"

"I'd feel better if LSU had beat Florida, but whatever," he said. "At least Florida's head coach got to have his moment. I'm glad for that. His wife looked really happy, too, so that's good, now hopefully, his son gets to take over as head coach," he continued.

Erika looked at her son confused as did AJ and Evie.

"Oh, you meant my hand and leg." Luke realized.

"Oh, my freaking god!" Evie exclaimed. "You're such a dork," she informed him.

AJ and Erika laughed.

"They're both good, I guess," he replied.

"Dr. Benjamin, when can we get the show on the road with PT?" Luke asked.

"Well," AJ began, "we have to let the swelling go down first but if all goes well, I'd imagine by the end of the week or early next week at the latest," he said.

"Cool, okay. Perfect," Luke responded. "Oh, and by the way, Doc, Evie told me that you don't think I'll play ball again, but I will. Like I told Evie, you have to tell my mom the worst-case scenario. I get that, but you don't know me," he boasted. "So, can I do my rehab at your place in Panama?" he asked.

Erika and AJ looked at each other.

"It looks pretty badass from the pics online," he said. "Eves also told me that my mom's into you," Luke blurted out, causing Evie to bury her face in a pillow she'd been clutching.

AJ smirked, trying to hide his amusement. Erika smacked Evie in the arm as her mouth dropped to the floor.

"Luke!" Erika exclaimed.

Ignoring his mother, Luke turned his attention back to AJ, continuing his reign of personal terror.

"I'm pretty sure that you're into my mom as well," he said. "I mean, you guys are older now, but since Eves told me that Mom hasn't been home in two days, it sounds to me like you both still got game," Luke said, seeming to enjoy the terror he was inflicting on his mother.

AJ, watching the look of despair on Erika's face, couldn't help himself any longer and burst into laughter. Evie was still hiding her face in the pillow, dying of laughter behind it.

"Have you lost your mind?" Erika asked him, still astonished by his behavior. "Do we need another CT scan because there's definitely wrong with you?" Erika half joked, trying to take the focus off herself and AJ.

"No, I just know that if I call it for what it is, I'll have a better chance of getting to Panama," he said. "Dr. Benjamin, I read about your sister. She made it to the Olympics after breaking her back. Your place is amazing, I've never seen anything like it," he insisted. "And neither have the reporters. There's like a million articles about you online."

Now Erika felt stupid. Her head had been in such a fog that she didn't even think to Google him. Her children obviously, didn't have that problem, she thought to herself somewhat sarcastically.

"Mom, Dr. Benjamin's place is the only chance I have to play ball again," Luke begged.

AJ agreed with Luke. He had thought about it before but figured there'd be no way that Erika would be open to the idea, except everything was different now. Luke was right, he needed a place like the compound. Now he just had to tell Erika that without her thinking he had ulterior motives. In this instance, his intentions were genuine and it was a win-win situation for him and Luke. He hoped she'd view it as a win for herself as well.

"Rik," AJ interjected, "Luke won't get here in the States what Dr. Pap and I have built, tweaked, and perfected in Panama. I'm not trying to sound arrogant, but there's a reason why the Olympians come to Panama," he reminded her.

"Has *everyone* lost their minds?" Erika asked. "No, Luke, we are not going to Panama," she declared. "We all have a life here, you, me, Evie. People don't just pick up and move to Panama, of all places," she said.

All three of them looked at her in sync, "Why not?" they exclaimed, staring at her. Erika was dumbfounded.

"Evie, it was only yesterday that you were angry with me, thinking that I might take off to Panama with him and today you're all for it?" Erika reminded her, baffled.

"I'm good if I get to go too," Evie responded. "Dr. Benjamin, can all three of us stay in Panama with you? Would you mind?" she asked.

"Of course," AJ responded. Turning to Luke next, AJ offered that Mitch was more than welcome to visit anytime and when he did, he'd always have a place to stay.

"Thanks, Doc! Hear that, Mom?" Luke asked, knowing she had.

Erika couldn't believe what she was hearing. "Yes, Luke. I heard him. Loud and clear," she assured. "Guys," she said, "I'd like to talk to Luke in private if I could, please."

Evie and AJ left the room. AJ brushed his hand across Erika's back as he left the room. He know if she were mad at him by her reaction to his touch. She looked up, locked eyes with him and smiled. He was relieved to be in the clear.

"Don't kill me, I'm an injured boy!" Luke begged his mother with a sly smile, unsure of how she was going to respond.

Erika sat down on the corner of her son's bed. "Luke," she began, "I want you to play baseball more than anything. I really do, but we just can't up and leave our lives here," she explained.

"Why?" he questioned further. "You hate the condo, and I know you enjoy real estate, but you worry about money all the time," he reminded his mother. "Just leave the condo, Mom."

"So, what's the plan, Luke? How long do we stay? A week, a month, a year, until you are able to play college ball?" Erika questioned, slightly annoyed by his blatant ignorance and inexperience. "Where do we live when we come back?" she asked, "If I walk away from the condo, it will ruin what little credit I rebuilt, and I won't be able to rent anything," Erika explained.

"Mom, you're being dumb."

"Excuse me," Erika responded, growing even more annoyed by this point.

Luke knew what he wanted to say but he'd already outed his mother enough this morning and wasn't sure how much more she'd let him get away with, injured or not.

"How did you and Dr. Benjamin first meet? Luke asked. "I mean I know it was in med school and stuff, but how?"

"It was still in undergrad. He annoyed the shit out of me," she responded, smiling thinking back to their first encounter in that adolescent evolutionary psychology class.

Luke could tell by the expression on his mom's face after just one question that he had her. All he had to do was ask the right questions and hello, Panama!

"And?" Luke pressured. "A lot of people annoy the shit out of you, but you don't end up spending two nights with them."

"Smartass, huh?" Erika laughed. "We debated about why women have smaller fingers than men. He said it was so we could pick berries for our men, and it was on."

"Oh my god! What? Ohhhh, I would have loved to have seen that smackdown," Luke said, imagining how ugly that must have gotten.

"Anyway," Erica continued, "I ran into him again in my first med school seminar, and I tried so hard to just ignore him, but I failed miserably," she said. "He baited me, and then dared me to debate him. I fell into the trap, and once again, we argued about the differences in bone structures between men and women. The class didn't know what to think," Erika said, smiling even bigger as she reminisced. "The next day, AJ came into class and told everyone that after more consideration, he felt I was correct and that he was in error. That was it. The friendship began."

"And you didn't know he wanted to get in your pants back then?" Luke asked, shocked. "Mom, guys are assholes. You know this. We don't make ourselves look like a dumbass in front of a bunch of people because we want another friend. No. It doesn't work that way," Luke said, unable to understand how his mother could be so naive.

Erika had to admit, Luke had a point.

"Mom," Luke began, "Do you remember that part in the movie, *Parenthood* where the son with the shitty-ass dad is walking off the race car track with his mother after Keanu almost kills himself racing?" Luke asked.

"I think so. Why?" Erika responded, unsure as to where their conversation was headed.

"Well, throughout the movie the son kinda treats his mom likes shit and favors the jerk dad even though his mom is always the one there for him. Her life is pretty crappy life and her kids totally take advantage of her, but as they're walking, the son asks his mom about her new boyfriend and if she really likes him. His mom says that she does because he does nice things for her and makes her happy. The son looks at his mom and tells her he's glad about that because she deserves for someone to be nice to her," Luke explained. "That's the way I feel when I see you and Dr. Benjamin together," he said. "I can see how happy you are, and you won't be if you're here and he's there. I mean, you hate men. You never date. Evie is your best friend, and now all of a sudden, you're staying out all night. It's awesome and I don't want that to end for you."

"Wow, Luke. I have to admit, you are good! Really good!" Erika joked, her eyes welling with tears.

"Thanks. Did it work?" he asked grinning, but she knew he was sincere. She didn't have any doubts about that.

"You get to tell your dad about this," she told Luke.

"So, we're going?" he screamed, almost jumping out of bed.

"Can we come back in?" AJ asked, as he and Evie worked their way back into Luke's room. "We heard a scream. Is everything all right?" he asked.

Luke was still waiting for his mother to respond.

"Yeah, we're good," Erika said, smiling. She turned to AJ and asked, "So, when do we leave for Panama?"

Evie jumped and Luke yelled "Yes!" loud enough to be heard on the next floor.

AJ smiled, walked over to Erika and hugged her. "Thank you," he whispered in her ear.

Panama

Mitch was less than happy to hear the news about Panama, but he understood that Luke was lucky to have such an opportunity. AJ and Mitch worked out a schedule for Mitch to visit, AJ offering to take care of all Mitch's travel expenses as well. Mitch was shocked by AJ's generosity, as was Erika, who wasn't crazy about all the money he was shelling out for this expedition. Without her knowing, AJ also took care of Erika's lease for the next twenty-four months. He had no intentions of her ever needing the condo again, but that would be a conversation for a later date. The next two days were busy packing up the condo and making preparations to transport Luke, which proved to be no easy feat. Ump Ted came by one more time to visit Luke before he left the hospital. They had a nice conversation and Luke promised to keep him updated about his progress and recovery.

The police also contacted Erika to let her know that they had Luke's assailant in custody and asked that she ID him before leaving. That was a huge weight off of everyone's shoulders, especially since the defendant was agreeable to taking a plea, versus putting everyone through a trial.

Admittedly, Erika was having the time of her life. She had forgotten what it felt like to walk hand in hand with someone or to be given a random kiss on the forehead. She loved how AJ stood next to her with his arm on her, either wrapped around her waist or over her shoulder. Erika laughed with him. She smiled all the time, and she looked forward to everyday now. Every moment was enjoyable, and she was getting more and more excited about their upcoming move. Erika was grateful to have a son who knew her so well and was able to be candid with her, otherwise she might not have agreed to the venture.

As she packed up the condo, Erika thought about how she had laid in bed just a couple of weeks earlier, feeling so dismayed about her life and such disdain towards every day. She hated to get out of bed, she hated the condo, and everything in her life reminded her of failure, but not anymore. Erika hadn't really told AJ everything about why she no longer practiced medicine. She wondered if he already knew because whenever she'd try, he'd tell her that none of that mattered to him. She was his "Rik," he'd tell her, and that's all he needed.

Erika hadn't slept much since deciding to move to Panama. Her mind was either too busy trying to process everything about Panama or her eyes were too busy watching AJ sleep. Erika was grateful to God for healing her son and her heart, and he did it all by sending an angel she'd met so many years before. She also realized that God did send her a sign the night she so desperately begged Him of one. It had been only seconds after she prayed that she heard AJ's voice for the first time in over twenty years.

Before Luke was released from the hospital, AJ took a few moments to thank the nursing staff and the other doctors for all their help with Luke. They all said their farewell to AJ, hugged Luke, and then some shot Erika a smirk with a wink as they left with the handsome doctor.

"Eat your hearts out, bitches," she muttered under her breath. It was her turn to be happy.

The trip was long, especially for poor Luke. AJ increased his pain medication so he could get through the trip. Fortunately, he slept most of the plane ride. Evie, on the other hand spent her time flirting with the young man seated next to her, also in route to Panama. Leave it to Evic to make plans for the weekend, in a new country, of which she knows nothing about. Erika was humored as Evie explained how they weren't able to pick a place to meet.

Luke chimed in, "Oh, gee, I don't know. Maybe it would be hard to pick a place when you've yet to ever step foot in the country," he said sarcastically.

Evie didn't help herself either when Luke asked her what the guy's name was and she couldn't remember. Even AJ was at a loss for words with that one.

Dr. Pap was anxiously awaiting their arrival. He was waving his hands, holding up a large white sign that read "Alex, hot chic, and her family" at the gate. In disbelief, AJ first shook his head and then his hand. Evie and Erika, feeling flattered and a little embarrassed shared are hug with the high-spirited doctor.

Dr. Pap turned to Luke, somewhat disappointed, "What, you're not going to get up and say hello to me?" he said, laughing wildly at his own joke.

Luke actually began to move forward, not thinking. He retuned Dr. Pap's gift of sarcasm, owning the last word.

"Sorry," Luke responded. "I don't get up for people who are already at eye level standing when I'm sitting. What would be the point?" he asked, grinning.

"Ha! That was good. I like that someone is with wit!" Dr. Pap admitted. "You're going to need it for when rehab kicks your ass, young man," he said patting him on the shoulder, slightly amused by his comeback.

"What is it with you guys and your contempt for short people?" AJ asked Erika, as if he were truly shocked.

Panama was warm, it was at least ninety-eight degrees when they landed. Fortunately, the breeze from the ocean helped. Evie exited onto the dock where they awaited a ferry to take them to the island of the Embera Tribe.

"Hello, sun!" Evie exclaimed. "Goodbye, shit-hole Michigan!"

Erika was nervous and didn't know what to expect once they landed on the island. AJ insisted they get settled at the compound first, and then go on to meet the tribal members later that evening. Erika had never seen anything like the compound before. She had pictured brick buildings and concrete, but it was more like a high-end campsite with a horse ranch. It spanned over a hundred acres and staff got around the compound by way of golf cart, or horseback. Erika looked at AJ in disbelief.

"We had to expand a bit after we began treating the Olympians," he explained, sheepishly.

"I guess so," Erika responded, patting him on the shoulder.

"Let's get Luke settled," AJ suggested.

"He asked to skip tonight. Did you know that?"

"I didn't, but I think that could be a good idea. If he has a chance to rest, he might change his mind, but if he's not sure that he'll be up for it, he should stay back. The tribal people are very active, let's just say, and Luke's already had more activity today than I would like." AJ admitted.

"I think it's important that he prioritize his activities, especially if he hopes to start PT tomorrow," he added.

"Whatever you say, boss," Erika laughed.

"Hey, can you say that to me in bed tonight?" AJ asked, feeling hopeful, shrugging his brow.

"If you can catch me," Erika challenged him, running off towards the ocean.

She couldn't wait to feel the water and the sand in her toes. She was the one with ulterior motives this time. Erika needed a moment alone with AJ, and she figured Luke could stand to wait just a few more minutes to get settled. They had been so busy packing, planning, and traveling that the new couple didn't have much alone time. Erika barely made it to the water when AJ caught up with her.

"Got ya!" he bragged coming up behind her, picking her up, and spinning her before setting her down again in front of him. There he stood, looking deeply in her eyes as he moved her wet hair out of her face.

"I can't wait to spend every day with you. I still can't believe you're here with me," AJ said catching his breath.

"You fell into my trap," Erika teased. "I needed a minute with you," she admitted, wiping the sand off of his neck.

"How about tomorrow, we wake up early and watch the sunrise over the ocean? How does that sound?" He asked, smiling as he spoke to her.

"Amazing."

Erika and AJ got Luke settled in his room, which happened to be the size of a small house. He'd be staying across the hall from them, at least for the time being. Luke was so exhausted from the day of traveling, he fell asleep and didn't hear Evie come in, freaking out about her amazing room.

"So, what else don't I know about you?" Erika asked, as she and AJ toured the rest of the compound.

"What do you mean?" he asked, sounding a little surprised. "You can ask me anything you want, I'm an open book."

"This is just a lot to take in," Erika said, looking across all the acres of villas, training and medical stations, and the horse stable with three of the most beautiful horses she'd ever seen. "I mean, this is a small city and the equipment here is just ridiculous. I can see why the Olympians want to come here, and I can only imagine what the tribes think. I'm just mind-blown," Erika confessed.

"You have to remember something, Rik, because I can already hear your wheels turning." "First of all, anything I have, is yours too, but don't compare what you see here to what you don't see in your own life," AJ reminded. "It's easy to put a price tag on the stuff here, but how much is the love of a child worth? It's immeasurable and infinite," he said smiling, swinging her hand as they walked. "I haven't been raising a son or taking in a broken young girl to raise whom you'd just met, but still took a risk and loved anyway." AJ looked at

Erika endearingly, "I've had grants and wealthy grandparents who contributed wonderfully to my work. You've rebuilt your life, a couple different times on your own with people needing so much from you when you had nothing left to give," he reiterated. "We both fix people, Rik. It doesn't matter what your title is, 'Mom,' 'Doctor,' 'Dr. Mom,' or whatever," he joked. "I heal with my hands, but you heal with your heart. Lives are better because of us, and now it is our time. Now is the time that we make our own lives better too just by loving each other."

"You're a smart guy, Dr. Benjamin." Erika said, feeling euphoric.

"I don't know about that. I picked that guy for a partner," pointing to Dr. Pap who was in the distance, pounding the air as if he were playing the drums, rocking out to an old Def Leppard song coming from one of the training centers.

Once he realized that AJ and Erika were watching him, Dr. Pap yelled out them, "The new Olympians must be here!" he said excitingly. Erika looked up at AJ, and all they could do was to roll their eyes.

Erika was disappointed that Luke wasn't up to meeting the Embera Tribe that evening. She was amazed by the people and the culture. Erika and Evie were introduced to a smaller village, one that had a little over a hundred people living in thirty-one houses on that part of the island. They didn't speak Spanish as Erika anticipated but instead spoke Embera or Cholo. They were hard workers but played even harder, chanting and dancing. They made beautiful art pieces and enjoyed hosting the doctors and their friends. Some of the women and children really took to Evie and Erika. AJ disappeared for a bit while Erika and Evie were taught how they prepare meals Embera style. Their meals consisted mainly of plantains, rice and maize, bananas, and of course, fish. The younger girls enjoyed braiding and twisting Erika and Evie's hair, and they smothered the American women with homemade gifts.

The sun had just started to set, and the Embera women finished cooking dinner over the fire, still fierce and going strong when AJ finally returned. Erika saw him walking towards them and many of the children ran to him, "Doctor, Doctor," they called out, waiting for their turn to hug him. Luke was with him. Erika went out to meet her special guys and to claim her hug.

"Hi, sweetie," she said to Luke. "How ya feeling, honey?"

"Great!" he said and both Erika and Evie thought he looked better too. "AJ said you were bumming that I wasn't here, and I always want to avoid the wrath of Mama Bear," he joked.

Admittedly, Erika was thrilled to see him.

"Thanks, babe," she said to AJ, sneaking in a kiss, causing quite the reaction from the natives.

The healers were very interested in Luke's injuries. AJ and Dr. Pap explained how the healers often took credit for their medical practices, but the docs agreed, too, the healers contributed to the overall healing process, especially with children.

AJ went over to look at a little boy sitting in his mother's lap while the other kids danced around. He looked very saddened, and his leg was deformed. Dr. Pap walked up to Erika, noticing that she had been staring at the little boy.

"That's Kunu, he's eight," Dr. Pap told her. "Alex has been researching the best way to repair his leg and part of his hip for almost two years now."

"Wow," Erika replied. "He looks like he's four or five at most," she said shocked.

"William Syndrome," Dr. Pap explained. "That's what we see the most of around here, syndromes and birth defects. These children don't get a lot of broken bones or injuries, especially not like the Olympians, but they're born with abnormalities, and we need to fix them. We spend a lot of time waiting until their bodies can handle the surgery," he continued. "Your friend," he said, referring to AJ, "is a very good doctor, but he's not great," Dr. Pap said, concerned.

Erika was about punch him out until she quickly saw the point Dr. Pap was trying to make.

"Alex is brilliant, he's very skilled, and the best I've worked with, but he's scared. With your son, he wasn't scared, and it was a thing of beauty to watch him work," he continued, nodding his head in agreement with himself, as if he were watching the event replay in his mind. "Your son's surgery was the first time in all the years I've worked with Alex that he took the much-needed risk. Alex likes to play it safe," Dr. Pap affirmed.

Erika thought about how AJ never married and had never told her how he felt all those years ago.

"Alex will search forever for the safest plan of action when a slightly riskier one is right in front of him, and better for the patient too. Alex is afraid of failing, that's what it is," Dr. Pap concluded.

Erika agreed.

"We all are," the wise doctor validated. "Unfortunately, though, unless you fail, and you feel the hurt of that failure, you never soar," he projected, looking up at Erika with a look of satisfaction on his face. He obviously knew what it felt to have that sense of accomplishment and pride.

Erika knew a lot about what Dr. Pap professed. With everything she'd been through over the past three years, and even longer, considering her failed relationships, she knew Dr. Pap was right. You learn what to do right the second time, or even the third time around, from what you did wrong the first time, Erika thought to herself.

Dr. Pap squeezed Erika's hand as he told her, "I hope you can help our friend, because he's ready to soar. He has been for a while now. Playing it safe is the kiss of death for a doctor," the wise, senior physician explained. "Even playing it safe will only last for so long. Many docs don't come back after a setback or a loss," he said, as if her were speaking prophecy.

"It would be a shame if that happened to our friend."

Dr. Pap thought that Erika might be the key to pushing AJ to the next level surgically and helping him feel more secure in his skill.

"Maybe you can talk to him," Dr. Pap suggested. "Kunu needs a procedure that requires a femoral rotation and complete lumbar fuse replacement. It would appear that you're a good motivator for him, Ms. Erika," he told her. "I'm a crazy old fool but I wouldn't have told you all this unless it was to do good and never harm," he vowed.

Erika believed that her lover's colleague spoke from the heart and had only the best intentions. "All I can do is encourage him, personally," Erika told him, standing her ground. "I'm okay with discussing this with him because I believe in him whole-heartedly, but I won't offer an opinion on a specific procedure. That's not my expertise, and it's not my place to tell him what to do," she told Dr. Pap sternly yet kindly.

"That sounds like a good plan, Ms. Erika. Thank you."

AJ walked over to where Erika and Dr. Pap had been conversing and razzed the flamboyant physician for flirting with his Rik.

"Oh my, never," Dr. Pap replied looking at them both. "No offense, Ms. Erika," he said to her quite genuinely, "but you have far too much class for my taste. I like my women a lot younger, very, very trashy, and even more wild," he said with a grin. "I like it when they slap my bottom and beg to ride my pony!" he told them as he sent them a wink, galloping off, smacking his own ass.

"That is one messed up little old Indian dude," Erika said, now for the second time since having met him not too long ago. She tried desperately to remove the mental image from her mind of Dr. Pap smacking his own ass, galloping away.

"Oh, trust me," AJ cautioned, "that was mild."

The couple walked towards the fire where the Embera were singing and chanting. The children ran and played, a few of them successful at getting Evie to give them a horsey-back ride. Everyone was enjoying themselves, especially Luke who had taken an interest in a nineteen-year-old gymnast, hoping to still be onward bound for the 2020 Summer Olympics. Erika smiled to herself as she watched them through the crackling fire, flirting and laughing as if they hadn't met only an hour before. In the distance, Erika saw another Olympian arrive to join in the festivities. On his shoulder hung the sweetest little monkey who quickly jumped down to play with a village Rottweiler as if they were best friends. She stared, awestruck as these two vastly different creatures chased and played together like young school children.

"If only human beings knew how to treat each other so kindly," Erika imagined.

"I don't think people are all that bad, Rik," he challenged.

"You've never been put in the position to see how rotten people can be. Aej, you live a very sheltered, fortunate life, and I love that I'm a part it, but I've learned that people react out of fear, even if they don't have to. People are so worried about being rejected, worried that they're going to be left behind by someone or someplace that they trample each other to prevent losing out. What people don't realize, is it's this 'kill or be killed' mentality that creates the fear in the first place."

"Rik, that was way too deep for a such a fun night. Maybe let your guard down, hit the reset button, consider giving the human race a second chance."

"The world is mean and selfish, AJ. Just ask Evie. To think otherwise is foolish."

"Rik," AJ spoke, genuinely and calm, "I'm sure I haven't seen or experienced what you have, and I have you now, so if I haven't seen the evil in the world yet, I'm not going to. Even if it exists, I'm not taking my eyes off of you long enough to notice anything else. But can you do something for me, please? Can you try to let love in? Not just from me, but from all around you. Maybe if you let it in, then you'll see the good in people as I do. I want nothing more for you than that."

"Yes, I will try, but only because you made me," she promised, sarcastically, the only way she could.

"You need to meet Doo-Doo," AJ announced. "Doo-Doo," AJ called out, followed by a whistle. The monkey was a regular playmate of the villagers and had become a close companion of his.

"You named the village monkey after poop!" Erika said, highly amused.

"It seemed appropriate," AJ defended, laughing so hard he could barely speak. "We gave him that name after he pooped on Pap!" AJ explained, pausing to hurl over once again until finally able to catch his breath. "Pap fell asleep under a tree that Doo-Doo was playing in and plop, there it was. Pap was *covered* in Doo-Doo's poop splatter. It was everywhere!" he said. "Oh my god, Rik, I wish you could have seen it! It was the funniest shit ever, literally and figuratively," AJ said, bursting out again at the joke he just made. "It was the only time I had ever heard Pap swear, and let me tell ya, he made up for lost time."

Erika was laughing almost as hard as AJ by that point, and even more so after he told her how the Embera people, who can't even speak English, had begun teasing Pap as well.

For months they would walk past him, call him Dr. Plop-plop and then run away laughing.

"Oh my god," Erika said, wiping away tears from her eyes, having laughed so hard. "Yep, I'd have to agree with you, babe. Doo-Doo is the perfect name for him," Erika said, as Doo-Doo, still hanging on, AJ smiled widely at her before returning to his buddy, the Rottweiler.

Erika doubted she could be serious after having such a fun evening, especially having heard the poop story. She figured she'd use the golf cart ride back to their villa to get a feel for AJ's demeanor regarding Kunu's condition. She was curious to hear how he expected the surgery to go, and when, for that matter.

"Who was that little boy you were looking over?" Erika asked AJ feeling slightly guilty for the question since she already knew the answer, having conversed with Dr. Pap, or Dr. Plop-plop as the Embera call him.

"Oh, that's Kunu," he replied. "That little boy is in so much pain," AJ began, saddened. "I feel so badly for him," he admitted. He explained that Kunu's bones are so frail and weak that nothing can be done until they strengthen.

"There's nothing that can be done now?" Erika asked.

"No, not really, the problem is that he needs the cortico-steroids he takes to bring down the inflammation, in order to reduce the pain..." Erika interrupted, finishing AJ's sentence.

"What helps him also hurts his because the steroids weaken his bones."

"Exactly."

"What about Dr. Pap? Has Dr. Pap had experience with any other advanced procedures that he could assist you with and that just might be appropriate for Kunu?" Erika questioned. "What I mean to say is, could the two of you work together, even if another procedure entails more risk? Can you do for Kunu like you did for Luke?" she prodded.

"Luke was a unique case," AJ quickly replied.

"Why so?" Erika shot back, not letting AJ off the hook. "If I wasn't his mother, would you have gone the way of the AcuPac?"

"Probably not," he said.

Erika didn't say anything more until they arrived at the villa and were settled in bed.

Reaching out for his face and turning it inward to hers, she said, "I know it's easy to self-doubt. Trust me, I've written the book on that, but I also know that you're an amazing surgeon. My God, AJ, look at all you've done for your patients. Look at this place, the entire compound, look all around you," Erika directed. "This little boy needs you to step outside your comfort zone, and I know Dr. Plop-plop will support you a hundred percent," she insisted with a little humor to lighten the mood. "Maybe, we both have some things we need to open our minds up to, Aej."

"You're right. I know you're right," AJ conceded, moving in closer to Erika and beginning to kiss her from the neck downward. "I'll talk to Pap in the morning," he promised, while still moving his mouth downward, "if, and only if, we can ride the horses out onto the beach to see the sunrise," he coaxed her.

Just as Erika was about to respond, AJ positioned her legs around his neck and began to please her. His tongue was magical, and all Erika could do was to squirm with pleasure. She never did respond to his ultimatum, and they spent their entire first night in Panama making love, with the sound of the ocean in the background.

PT Boot Camp

Erika had never seen a sunrise so beautiful. Of course, she knew that being with AJ made all the difference. Erika rode a white horse, more beautiful than any she'd ever seen and AJ's a lighter brown, just as beautiful as the morning sky. The horses grazed nearby as the couple enjoyed their first morning in Panama together. They laid on the beach with the tide creeping up on them, with sand embedded in their toes. In between their passionate moments, they discussed Luke's PT which would be starting later that day.

AJ thought a lot about what Erika would do once Luke was able to return to the States for school and hopefully to play baseball as well. Would she and Evie return with Luke or would Erika want to stay with him, and then would Evie be okay with staying there while her brother was so far away? There were so many variables that AJ couldn't control, and that worried him. He knew it be a long while before he could return to the States for any significant period of time. He still had Kunu to care for which required that he stay in Panama to monitor him before and after his surgery. It would be several months before Kunu would be ready for surgery, regardless of what surgical procedure AJ went with. He also had several others in need of his care as well. AJ felt sick at the idea of not having his Rik there beside him every day. He wanted to marry Erika. He wanted her to be his wife more than anything else in the world. He knew it was too early to ask her to now, having just arrived in Panama, and Luke's therapy just beginning, but AJ planned on asking her very, very soon.

Luke began PT as scheduled. He suspected that AJ was behind the purposeful partnering of him with Jessie Galow, the nineteen-year-old Olympian he had met the day before. Jessie had broken her femur and torn her ACL while doing a dismount from the uneven bars, but she was not going to give up her dream of making it to Tokyo in 2020. The first day was a lot harder than Luke expected. He had a physical therapist and two personal trainers working with both him and Jessie that were more like boot camp drill sergeants than medical civilians. Jessie was all about their militaristic style, but Luke had never been exposed to such intense training. Up until now, Luke worked with high school or travel ball coaches who were nothing like what he was up against now. Everything came naturally for him, and he had it very easy up until now.

Jessie, on the other hand, had been working her whole life in hopes of making it to the Olympics. It was do or die for her. Jessie's training had always been difficult. Her coaches had always been intense, and unlike baseball for Luke, gymnastics wasn't natural for her. She had to work her ass off twice as hard, and it took her double the amount of time to master the same skill as other gymnasts. She couldn't wait to get started, and Luke just wanted to run away.

AJ stopped in the training center to see how the first day was progressing. He admitted to Luke that he did indeed purposefully pair him up with Jessie, but not for the reasons Luke had first assumed.

"Luke, there is no way I would ever give you a training partner to help you score a girlfriend," AJ laughed. "I'm all for helping your baseball game, and that's the only game I care about. You're going to have to score your own game with her outside of rehab," AJ said smirking.

Luke was confused.

"My dear young Luke," AJ began, "I paired you with Jessie because out of everyone here working towards their goals, she's the most unlike you and that will work to your advantage. Give it time and you'll see what I mean," he said.

Luke took a five-hour nap once his first day was done and over with. Jessie, on the other hand, continued to train on her own for another two hours, helping the villagers with their manual labor. When he woke, Luke was upset and told

Erika that he was done and that AJ set him up to fail. Erika, having had her ass kicked by life, knew better. She knew that the greatest challenges nurtured success and finding the ability to overcome nurtured life itself.

"I really doubt that AJ took us out of our own environment, had us all completely change our lives, and reinvent ourselves in a foreign country, no less, because his long-term goal was for you to fail," she pointed out.

Luke knew he was overreacting and that his mother was right. Jessie appeared at his door, "Hey, want to go for a walk or a roll for you?" she asked.

Luke was still wheelchair or scooter bound until his leg was strong enough for a walking cast. His hand wouldn't support his weight for crutches, especially being that his hand was the most severe of his injuries.

"Sure," Luke agreed.

Jessie asked him if he felt strong enough to allow her push him, to which he responded in a serious tone, "Sure, I think I can handle it," causing Erika to laugh aloud upon overhearing their conversation. Luke finally got it that Jessie was really ripping on him by asking if he felt strong enough to let *her* do all the work. He shot his mom a scowl as Jessie wheeled him out.

On their stroll, Jessie talked about how excited she was to get back to PT and training the next day. Luke asked her if she "sees dead people too," insinuating that she had lost her mind. Luke suddenly figured out what AJ was trying to do by pairing him with Jessie. He was trying to motivate him. To his jab, Jessie went full force into the painful truth.

"I think its crazier to work your whole life for something, almost get there, and then see everything you've worked for almost vanish right in front of your eyes, just to get an opportunity for a second chance by coming to this place and to not take advantage of every minute of it."

"Dr. Benjamin said that you were determined to get back to playing baseball, LSU, wasn't it? Then onto the pros?" she asked.

Luke nodded.

"Then you better accept that the next several months of your life are going to be really hard, and you better hope they are so when you do get back out on that mound, you'll know you deserve to be there," Jessie said. "Regret is the worst feeling in the world, and if you don't change how you think right now, you will fail, you won't make it, and you won't play ball. It's as simple as that," she said, adamantly. "Do you know how many times I've failed? Hell, I broke my leg in front of two thousand people during a pre-Olympic game last year. I know this is the first time you've hit a road block, and I mean a real road block, not just losing a game or something stupid like that, but you did," she said as they approached the horse stable. "So, you can complain about how hard PT is or you can see what real success feels like when you walk back on that ball field. That's when you and the rest of the world will know that you're the real deal," she said.

Luke recalled a conversation he had similar to this with Ump Ted on the day of the accident. He knew that the accident happened for a reason and had he not been put in the position to finish something hard, he probably wouldn't end up finishing anything worth something at all.

"Now, we are going to go horseback riding," Jessie declared. "I am going to work the hell out of this leg, not to mention my ACL, by riding that beautiful horse over there, and you are going to sit behind me," she said, not really allowing Luke a choice in the matter. Jessie helped Luke out of the wheelchair, and they used the lift that AJ installed in the barn for situations like this. To Luke's surprise, Jessie boarded the horse with ease.

"Don't worry, we're going to go slow," she said. "Wrap your arms around my waist and use your right forearm to hold you," Jessie advised, knowing that he wouldn't be able to use his right hand.

Luke enjoyed his ride with Jessie. They didn't talk anymore about PT or injuries, but instead got to know each other better personally. Luke was shocked to learn that Jessie had tutors and was mostly home schooled, or hotel schooled since most of her education was while she was on the road, either training or competing. Jessie explained that home schooling was really her only option given her training and travel schedule. They talked about their parents and Luke felt grateful to have both of his, and now AJ in his life as well. Jessie's dad died in Afghanistan when she was twelve, and her mom worked two jobs in order to pay for gymnastics. Jessie's voice saddened when she admitted that her mother really wasn't around much in her teen years, but she understood that her mom was only absent so she could provide for her and not because she didn't care. Luke listened to every word she said. He had been humbled that afternoon and decided that he was going to go into PT the next day ready to work.

Erika helped Luke into the villa and to his room at the end of the hall. She didn't ask him how it went with Jessie that afternoon, but she didn't need to.

Luke saw AJ out of the corner of his eye and yelled out, "Thank you, AJ. You were right, AJ," in a snarky tone.

"You're welcome, Luke. I'm always right, Luke," AJ responded laughing, reflecting on just how much kids his age have left to learn.

Erika knew that all had gone well. She returned to the bedroom where AJ already was and took off her robe. Underneath, she wore a very revealing nighty that she'd bought just before she left for Panama. Erika thought she should properly thank him for looking out for her son. As she let her nighty fall off her body, AJ stared, entranced in the beautiful woman before him.

"You don't just win your way into a mother's heart by being kind to her children," Erika said, climbing into bed. "You also win your way into their, well, you know," she said as she headed south after licking his face and began pleasing him orally.

Erika and Evie spent a lot of time during those first two months in the Embera Village. They helped with gathering food, cooking, washing, and caring for the children. Erika enjoyed working in the village. She was closer to AJ, and she loved watching him interact with the children, both as a doctor and as their friend. Dr. Pap was believed to be a medicine man and went through the village routinely while AJ tended to the surgical cases. Dr. Pap had operated on many, many serious cases within the village and in the States. By comparison, he was more experienced than AJ. He was also older and, despite the fact that he acted like a twenty-year-old gigolo, Dr. Pap was seventy-two and his eyes were beginning to fail him. He still assisted AJ, but only with the most difficult cases. AJ had mentioned to Erika on more than one occasion that Dr. Pap grew tired much easier than he had in the past.

Everyone seemed to have found their purpose in Panama. Evie went between the village and the compound, hanging out with some of the Olympians and had struck up a nice relationship with Joel, another Tokyo-bound Olympian. Luke was perpetually with Jessie. The "get your shit together speech" she gave him early on really helped him to get his head straight and stay focused on the end goal, baseball. They followed their treatment plan perfectly, and Luke was walking without assistance after only six weeks into rehab. His hand was more stubborn than his leg but was still improving, just at a slower pace. Luke didn't allow himself to get down about it, instead he would repeat, "It's all about the goal" to himself as he trained.

Mitch had come to visit twice in the recent couple of months and was a huge support for his son, cheering on his progress and encouraging him to keep pushing forward. Jessie, too, had made incredible progress but it was still too soon to know how her leg would react to the impact of a dismount. She had more work to do. Outside of rehab, Luke and Jessie were normal teenagers and spent time exploring various parts of Panama. Luke was never so happy to be able to walk again, commenting on how he had a new appreciation for all the abilities he had taken for granted. Luke and Jessie denied that they were anything more than just friends, but Erika and AJ knew how that worked and called bullshit when either of them would regard the other as "just a friend." As for AJ and Erika, every day was better and better. Neither of them had ever been so happy. AJ decided that it was time to make her his wife.

AJ loved his work, especially when he was able to see the fruits of his labor. He'd hoped Kunu would have been further along by now and ready for surgery, but he wasn't even close. The good news was, Dr. Pap had found a medication cocktail that helped tremendously with Kunu's pain. Erika stared smiling as she watched AJ, who was watching Kunu. It was the first time he felt well enough to play with the other children. Kunu wasn't able to walk but he was engaged in the game from his wheelchair. One of the other children even wheeled him closer and another picked him up so he could dunk the ball in the net. The other children cheered for him, and Kunu clapped for himself. When Erika noticed that AJ was crying, she went and wrapped her arms around him from the back. She could tell by how hard he squeezed her that the love he felt for that little boy was infinite.

"I love you," she told him, reaching up to kiss his cheek. He turned to her, and she wiped away an isolated tear.

"And I you, my Rik," he responded, kissing her lips. The children noticed them together and stopped their game. They started clapping for them and even Kunu made a kissing motion with his mouth, teasing them.

"Yeah, yeah," AJ said waving them away, and the Embera children resumed their game.

The Embera villagers were preparing for a magnificent celebration later that evening. A ten-year-old boy from the village had separated from his mother the day before and after a day of worrying and chanting in prayer, he was returned to them by a tribal member form another village. AJ decided he was going to take advantage of the celebration and ask Erika to marry him. She wouldn't suspect anything, as she, too, had gone looking for the young boy and was just as elated and ready to celebrate his return.

AJ let Dr. Pap in on his intention to marry Erika weeks ago, who in turn *told* him that it would be he who would marry them and that the ceremony would be on the beach. Dr. Pap actually proved to be an old romantic and gave AJ some surprisingly great ideas about the proposal and wedding. Dr. Pap heard Evie sing to one of the Embera children who'd gotten hurt and was crying. He told her that she was a beautiful songbird. Evie was touched by his compliment, and Dr. Pap was touched by her kiss on the cheek.

Dr. Pap had the perfect song in mind, and he would soon ask her to learn *I Choose You*, so the songbird could bless the couple with her angelic voice at the wedding. He wondered if

Evie would do it or if she'd be too anxious. He wanted to ask her, but not yet. Dr. Pap felt honored that AJ trusted he alone with the secret and he would not let his friend down. Dr. Pap asked the village women to make rings for them to exchange, three in total. One to ask and two to vow. Dr. Pap drew what he wanted them to make. Dr. Pap took over, trusting that his friend would allow him to do so. He took an online class to be able to marry them, and then gave AJ the receipt for $320 he had to front for the class.

"Sure, Pap," he said, shaking his head. "No problem, old buddy, but did I ask you to marry us?" he joked.

"You two wouldn't even be together if it weren't for me!" Dr. Pap boasted.

AJ decided to play along. "You know what, Pap, I'm sorry, please forgive me for not being more appreciative. Of course, Erika and I wouldn't have fallen in love had it not been for you and the Diamondback Saloon. I hope one day we can properly express our gratitude," he said.

Dr. Pap appreciated the validation he deserved until he realized the AJ was playing him.

"You little rat!" he said.

"Oh, Pap. I love ya, buddy. You make everyday fun, you know that?" AJ asked, patting him on the shoulder.

Dr. Pap looked back at him, "Of course, I know that," he said straight faced, offended that AJ might think otherwise.

AJ sought the assistance from one of the tribal elders to help him arrange the perfect proposal. Now, more than ever before, AJ was thankful he had learned enough Choco to communicate with the Embera.

The nighttime sky was perfect. There was a hint of rain in the air dancing upon thick clouds, and a constant breeze that was just enough to send a chill in the face of the raging afternoon sun about to set as if to take a break from its wrath. The sky was a mix of blue and pink, nothing he had ever seen before in over ten years he'd lived in Panama. It was as if the heavens were painting the perfect picture for them.

Laughter rang over the crackling fire. The young boy was lifted up in exaltation for having returned. Erika and Evie danced around the fire holding hands, while Luke and Jessie held hands as well, but under the privacy of the grass hut a short way away from where the fire danced. Kunu sat alongside his mother, still feeling well enough to clap and partake in the festivities. The Embera were outlined in Jagua body paint to show thankfulness, joy, and celebration. AJ watched as his Rik illuminated the night. She was so beautiful and soon she'd be his wife.

Dr. Pap came up beside AJ, and to remain inconspicuous, he slipped the first of the three rings the Embera women had made in AJ's pocket.

"Now, all she has to do is say yes," Dr. Pap said. "You're really going to look like a dummy if she doesn't," he walked away laughing. His laughter seemingly increasing the further he walked from AJ. Dr. Pap looked back at his friend and realized that AJ had taken him seriously as he stood frozen in place. Dr. Pap quickly returned to his friend to reassure him that he was only teasing and that of course Erika was going to say yes.

"Pap, I don't know," AJ realized, looking pale and then in utter panic, he began rambling to Dr. Pap. "I mean, we still hadn't discussed what was going to happen when Luke went home, and he's going to," AJ stuttered through his sentence. "He's going to be able to play ball, and I'm happy for him, but I don't know if Erika will stay or go. I can't leave yet because I have to help Kunu, and Evie might leave too and go back home with Joel and—"

"My friend, my friend," Dr, Pap interrupted, "A mother never leaves her children, but she allows them to leave her, so they may lead their own lives and find their own loves," the wise physician assured. "Luke and Evie are doing well, they're healing and they're thriving. Just like the Embera, they are much better because of you, and look at Ms. Erika," he directed. "That beautiful woman had a heart of stone until you filled it with love. She will say yes, my friend, she will say yes," assured the Medicine Man.

"Thanks, Pap." AJ said, feeling beyond grateful to his mentor.

"Are you sure you want to officiate?" AJ asked. "You should be my best man because you really are, Pap. You're the best man I've ever had the blessing of knowing and working with."

"Of course, I'm going to marry you, you fool. You already paid $320 so you 'get this' all ceremony long," he joked pointing to himself as if he were a playboy porn star.

AJ laughed in disbelief of his friend.

"Luke should stand next to you as your best man," Dr. Pap advised, and with another dose of insight, he proceeded to explain why. "Luke has been her best little man, and then her best young man, and now her best product of a man beginning since the day he was born. He can stand now, next to you as your best man because the two of you helped him to stand when he couldn't and rise when it would have been easy to fall. Luke will stand next to you as a symbol of his willingness to share the most special person in his life with you, and it's only right that he has the best seat in the house next to you and his mother."

Staring once again at is friend in disbelief, but this time for a much different reason, AJ responded, "Pap, I'm going to tell everyone your secret," he said.

"My secret?" Dr. Pap asked.

"Yep, that you have a huge heart," AJ confirmed.

Dr. Pap, with his mischievous grin couldn't help himself. "Ah, Alex buddy, if you really want to help this old dog out? You'll tell those young Olympian ladies that I have a huge….,"

"No, no, no, oh no. My god, Pap. You were old when they were born!" AJ reminded him.

"I knnnoooowww! Hubba, Hubba!" the dirty old man responded, raising his eyebrows.

AJ went to prepare for his big moment. He pulled out the ring that Dr. Pap had slid into his pocket. The Embera women amazed him and Dr. Pap was a genius. Dr. Pap's design was remarkable. The ring was clear glass with a white swirl in the middle shaped into an infinity symbol encased in white gold. It was the most beautiful thing AJ had ever seen and it was exactly her style. The Embera women decorated AJ's face with Jagua body paint, customary for any ceremony. A wedding proposal such as AJ had planned didn't exist in the Embera culture, but to them, it was a ceremony, deserving of their honorable custom. AJ took a moment to freshen up and it was time.

Erika turned her head just in time to watch AJ walk down the steps to where the festivities were. She ran out to him, "Your paint looks fantastic!" she said, checking it out. She had assumed it was in celebration of the young boy's return. "C'mon," she said to him, pulling him in the circle next to she and Evie.

In response to Dr. Pap's urging, Luke and Jessie joined in as well. Erika was unsure what was happening, but she was suddenly in the middle of the circle and the focus was on her. In the beginning, AJ stayed in the circle, dancing around her with everyone else. Erika was clueless. The Embera women began to twirl around her and the chanting grew louder until AJ stepped out of the circle and stood in front of her, as the singing and chanting continued.

"I told them that you can't resist a dare so today we are going to play a little game," he teased her.

"A game," Erika said looking unamused.

"Yes," he said. "I dare you to trust me," he said, blindfolding her.

"AJ, I swear to God, I'm going to kill you. What are you doing?" she whispered to him, trying not to make a scene or embarrass them.

"You're not trusting, since when do you pass on a dare, Rik?" he questioned her, grinning.

"Okay, okay, I will trust now and kill you later," she told him.

"Sounds good, Rik. Stick with that and I'll let you kill me later," he said, both of them laughing this time. "I dare you to walk with me," he directed, taking her hand and leading her down a path that seemed to go on forever, especially blindfolded with no clue as to where she was going. He led her to the edge of the Embera village, where the ocean met the sand. They walked, and the Embera women followed, throwing flower petals around the couple.

Erika was unsure of the scent that was in the air. "What is that?" she asked AJ.

"You'll see," he told her, then dared her to fall backwards.

"Fall backwards? Wait, what?" she exclaimed as he pulled her backwards and they fell on a silk cloth, supported by four Olympian friends that had been waiting silently on the beach for them.

Alongside the Olympians, quietly stood Evie and Joel and Luke and Jessie, who had just been let in on what was happening by Dr. Pap, who also stood alongside watching his dearest friends.

"Oh my God, AJ, what is this?" Erika pressured, her voice somewhere between happy and angry.

"We're almost to the really hard part, Rik, we're almost there," he repeated. "Just two more dares and you will be the champion of dares. I'll even give you a plaque that says so," AJ mocked, humorously.

"Ha-ha, you're a riot and a lunatic, Aej."

"Maybe, but this lunatic loves you," he said. "Rik, I dare you to climb onto that horse next to you."

Erika paused, trying to catch her breath, and in between her laughter and disbelief, she made sure she heard AJ correctly. "You want me to climb onto a horse, while I'm on some weird cloth thing, suspended in air by God knows what?" she asked.

"Yep, you got it. You know this horse, Rik. It's okay and you're up high enough. You can do it. I dare you!" he urged.

"Of course, I can do it!" she assured him, slightly annoyed by the insinuation that she couldn't.

"Okay, okay, I believe, I believe!" AJ laughed.

Erika reached out and felt for her steed. Once she found her balance, she was able to climb up onto the beauty with ease. "Ok, I'm up, I'm good," she said. "AJ?" she called out.

"I'm here, Rik." he comforted her as he boarded his own, saddled backwards on his horse so he could see her as their horses stood side by side. "Last dare, I told you though, this is the really hard one, so I want to make sure you're ready."

"I'm ready, Aej," she said, her face beaming. "This is kinda fun, strange, but fun," Erika said, finally letting go and trusting AJ.

"Good! I'm glad you're having fun because I have fun with you every day. I have fun every time I see you smile, I have fun every time I wake up with you next to me, and I have fun every time I hear you say my name, even angrily when Pap makes me do stuff that gets me in trouble," AJ joked, slightly looking over at his friend, who in turn was rolling his eyes.

Erika laughed hysterically. "So true," she said. "That little man makes you his bitch," she said, trying to compose herself, still having no idea that their friend was nearby.

AJ just about fell off his horse thinking how it must be killing Dr. Pap to not respond. Finally settled, he knew it was time.

"I'm going to reach over and take off your blindfold, okay, Rik," AJ told her, his hands shaking.

Erika looked all around her. She saw her children and Dr. Pap, the Embera women, and all the flower petals they placed on their path and all around them. Then she looked up at AJ sitting across from her. They each had the same horse as their first morning on the beach together. Under the beautiful pink and blue sky, Erika returned her attention back to AJ who moved up closer to her. He pulled out the glass ring and held it up in his palm. Erika gasped. Her eyes filled with tears and she held her hand over her mouth. Evie and Luke moved closer together as they watched their mother's reaction, wiping away tears of their own. Dr. Pap watched with a gentle smile and he felt proud to be a part of such a magical moment.

"Rik, I dare you." AJ began. "I dare you to love me every day, even if I get scoliosis and shrink," he humored her. "I dare you to tell me every time you're sad so I can make it better, and I dare you to let me do *all* the dishes and *all* the laundry so you don't have to. I dare you to smack me when I'm snoring and to spoon me when I'm not. I dare you to forgive me when I'm stupid and reward me when I'm not," he said with a smirk. "Most of all, Rik, I dare you to let me be the lucky one, the one that's gets to call you my wife, and if you say yes that you'll marry me, I swear to you and I promise you that I will make you happy for the rest of your life."

Erika couldn't speak. She couldn't move. She still held her hands paralyzed against her mouth.

Laughing, AJ said to her, "Rik, let me help you, honey," touched by the sincerity of her reaction. "Hold out your left hand if I can put my promise to you on your finger." Before he was done with the sentence, she shot her hand out to him and everyone broke into laughter. Erika's hand was shaking, but AJ successfully placed the ring on her finger, then pulled her onto his horse with him. Once she was in his arms, Erika was finally able to say the word yes.

August 16th

Erika woke up with the morning breeze coming in her window. She could hear Luke and Jessie in the kitchen trading laughs in between telling each other to "shh" so they wouldn't wake the newly engaged couple. Erika looked at her finger, still in disbelief. What was originally unbelievable joy and excitement ran though her as pure panic.

"Have I lost my mind?" she said quietly but loud enough to cause AJ to stir. She sat up in bed, lost in thought until she heard the shower running. Assuming they had both left, Erika put on her robe and headed towards the kitchen. She was surprised to see Luke there, fumbling around in the kitchen, still unable to do much with his right hand.

"Hi, honey," she said.

"Oh, hey, Ma. Sorry, I didn't mean to wake you," he said. "Jessie's in the shower and I wanted to surprise her with breakfast," he continued.

"Funny," she replied, I came out here to do the same thing for AJ and you didn't wake me up."

"Here," Erika said, signaling to him, "Let me help you."

"Thanks, Ma."

"Of course, I'm happy to help you make breakfast for all your 'friends,'" she said grinning.

"Whatever," Luke replied, rolling his eyes.

"So," Erika began, "How long did you know about last night?" she asked.

"Honestly, Ma, Evie and I both found out about it as Dr. Pap whispered what was about to happen in our ear *as* we followed both of you down the beach. We thought AJ really had lost his mind coming out with that war paint on," he laughed.

"I think he did lose his mind," Erika responded.

"Ut oh." Luke came closer, now sitting at the island across from where his mother was cooking. "Ma, you're not going be that chic in the *Runaway Bride* movie, are you?" he said jokingly until Erika didn't respond. "Mom! Tell me! Mom, I know you're like a book, a big book with large print that comes with an audiotape," he reminded her, laughing.

Erika always told Luke the same thing when her "mom radar" went off and she knew something was wrong.

"I don't know, Luke," Erika said, trying to identify what it was she was feeling so she could talk to him candidly. "I'm not very good at relationships, honey, and once you put a title on things, at least for me, they seem to spontaneously combust," she said, making an explosive sound with her mouth.

"You're funny," he said, shaking his head.

"What?" Erika replied in reaction to his response.

"Do you hear the reality behind what you're saying?" he questioned her. "You're going to break that man's heart because you're afraid he might break yours or that shit is going to get all jacked up again because of a title. So, in order to avoid potential pain, you're going to cause definite pain and still think things won't get jacked up? Besides," Luke continued, "He's not dad or that loser creep-o-criminal doctor. You and AJ are different, and you're going to have to stop trying to micromanage your life in order to avoid shit 'cause you might avoid some shit, but you'll make different shit and none of it will be enjoyable. Trust yourself, Ma. You're not the failure that you think. I thought you had learned that by now," Luke said, slightly irritated by his mother's lack of faith in herself.

"So did I," AJ said, after hearing them talking as he walked down the hall.

Taking the breakfast Erika made, Luke piled the two plates, one on top of the other, and scurried out of the kitchen. "And I'm outta here. Better check on Jessie," he said.

Erika was embarrassed that AJ had heard at last part of their conversation. "Hey, babe," she said, wrapping her arms around his neck then kissing him.

"Rik, are you okay?" AJ asked, trying to mask his hurt for concern.

"I'm fine, sit and eat with me," she told him, grabbing her coffee and Baileys. He wasn't going to let her change the topic.

"Hey, Rik. I expected you to be scared. I expected this reaction the day after a hundred percent," he admitted.

"You did?" she asked, confused.

"Yep, ask Pap." he said. "In fact, right before I went to freshen up, Pap had to talk me down because I was scared you'd say no. Not because you don't love me. I know you do, but because of the unknowns and, yes, even the 'marriage title effect' but, especially not knowing where the kids will end up in a month or a year," he explained.

"What did Dr. Pap say?" Erika asked, curious.

"To use your words, he is an odd little man," AJ concurred, standing again and wrapping his arms around Erika while smiling. "But he was right. He reassured me that we all, the kids, you, and me, we will find a way to stay in each other's lives and that situations will work themselves out if we allow them to. He also said he could see that your heart has softened and that with me is the best place it could be," AJ told her, staring lovingly at her.

Erika couldn't argue with that. Dr. Pap was right. Erika felt better. Their conversation helped her to feel validated but even more so, comforted.

She looked at AJ. "I'm good," she said, "And I really can't wait to marry you and I mean that. Nerves are normal, but I want nothing more than to marry you," she repeated.

"Good, now come here," AJ told her, leading her to the opposite side of the kitchen and grabbing a long cloth napkin and a piece of tape. "Let's leave it to chance," he said, tying yet another blindfold and leading her to the calendar.

"Oh my god, you're certifiable," she told him, feeling giddy.

"Yeah, maybe just a little," AJ concurred, joking back with her. "Now," he said, spinning her, "This is just like when you were a kid, but instead of pinning the tail on the donkey, you're going to place the tape on the date you are going to marry the donkey, he-haw, he-haw. Okay, go for it," he told her.

Erika stammered to the calendar and placed the tape on August 16th, only three days away. "Three days from now," she said, shocked. "That is too soon. We need time to plan," she said panicked.

"Well, you could have turned the page," AJ reminded her, slightly poking fun. "I figured you just couldn't contain yourself any longer." It earned him a smack to the gut with a smile from his bride to be.

"You didn't tell me I could," she told him.

"I didn't think I had to," he countered, still laughing. "Ha-ha, look who's the jackass now, Ha-ha-ha," he carried on, earning him the evil eye from Erika. "Seriously though, it's all good. This date is meant to be. We left it to chance and chance forgot to tell you to flip the page so, August 16th it is," AJ concluded, sounding proud of having taken control over the situation. "Also," he said, "Evie is already working on the song Pap picked, and Pap already got his license to officiate, so we're good to go. Luke's going to be my best man, I already asked him last night. You should probably talk to Evie, though. I mean, I'm assuming she's going to be your matron of honor," AJ laid it all out, causing Erika to feel dizzy for the second time.

Erika paused and thought. "Actually," she said, "I'm just gonna go with it, I'm not asking any questions, and I'll wait to be blown away," Erika asserted. "I'm leaving everything up to chance," she proclaimed.

"That's my girl," AJ told her, still ignoring breakfast and leading her back to the bedroom.

AJ was up and out early the morning of August 16th, partially because he had a lot to do but also because he was very nervous. He didn't want Erika to see him like that, especially since he spent so much time in the bathroom. Erika on the other hand, was calm, jovial, and floated through her morning into the afternoon as if it was just typical day. Luke practiced his best-man speech and Evie rehearsed *I Choose You* for the hundredth time, hiding out from their mother and AJ so they wouldn't ruin the surprise. The ceremony was at 4:00 p.m. in a cabana on the beach outside of the Embera Village. The Embera women weaved flowers into Erika's hair and her dress was simple, free flowing in the wind. With her golden blonde hair, she was the picture of an angel. Erika was honored to have her children standing beside her, and she even had her fur baby, Max, that she missed every day, with her as well. She wore a necklace with his pawprint engraved in it to keep him close to her heart. She was ready to go.

Dr. Pap proved that he can clean up well, wearing a new double breasted suit for the special occasion. He had also surprised them with a honeymoon in which they never expected to take, at least not now. They would tour for twenty-one days, traveling through Europe, of which Erika had never been, and their last nine days would be spent laying on the beach in Maui, the perfect honeymoon destination. He had arranged the flights, hotels, and their transfers, and he even arranged for tour guides on their behalf. He presented his gift to them at dinner the night before fand they were blown away by his gesture. AJ couldn't help but tease Dr. Pap about being stingy over $320 for the class he took in order to marry them, but then he spends thousands on their honeymoon.

"You're a puzzle, Pap. You are certainly a puzzle," AJ repeated. Dr. Pap also offered to take over caring for Kunu in AJ's absence, in addition to the less serious patients AJ had been monitoring. Erika asked him why he was so generous, but the man who was quite the mystery, simply responded that it was his pleasure.

Luke was handsome and Erika stunning, but none was so beautiful to her at that moment as her husband to be, waiting for her at the ocean's end, down an isle of white. If Erika had written her perfect day in a fairytale, today would still be better. Dr. Pap nailed it having Evie sing, *I Choose You.* She was a true songbird and the words expressed everything that AJ and Erika felt.

Erika walked slowly, arm and arm with Luke.

"I love you, Mom, I'm so happy for you," Luke whispered to her as he gave her hand to AJ and took his place next to him. Erika was already crying as she walked towards AJ, and then she cried even more when she saw Luke fist bump the air and tap his heart twice at Evie. It was his way of telling her he was proud of her. The friends and family who attended the ceremony were the people who meant the most to the couple. They were the people they saw every day, loved every day, and cared for every day. The Embera tribe paid respect to the traditional marriage ceremony and watched as their friends wed, even if they didn't understand all the words, they felt what was being said.

The moment was all Erika's and AJ's, but Dr. Pap stole the hearts of everyone watching as he spoke about the special couple.

I met a young Dr. Benjamin over ten years ago now in Costa Rica. Believe it or not, he told me about his "Rik" the very first day we met. True, by that time, they hadn't seen nor talked to one another in five or ten years since life took them in different directions, as life often does, but she was still hiding in his heart, just waiting until he found her again. As we took a moment to talk, I told him I was on a hunt for women half my age and he laughed at my quick wit. He told me that he just wanted a change of scenery in which to work. What a nerd! I thought to myself. No wife, no girlfriend? I couldn't even imagine how that could be. No, he told me, just his work. Then I asked him if there'd ever been a Mrs. Dr. Benjamin and again he replied no. This time though, he told me that he was in love once. She was "my Rik," he told me, but she never knew it because he never told her. I quickly understood why. In his eyes, I saw such a saddened soul. I saw that same saddened soul when I first met Ms. Erika. She kept me at arm's length, not sure what to think, which isn't uncommon. Most people don't know what to think about me. This was a different type of distance. It was a distrusting distance. She wasn't going to let anyone into her world until she knew for sure that she could.

Then something amazing happened one evening. They both let go. He stopped running and she didn't push away. They didn't have to protect themselves any longer. Her AJ and his Rik held the key to unlocking each other's hearts and opening the door to a whole new world for both of them. What a world is it! Love had transformed this couple. What started twenty years ago picked right back up where it left off that wonderful night when fate finally found them. You see, miracles do happen. Fate might takes us the long way home sometimes and might even take a turn we think we'll never recover from, until we do. We learn that we have to feel hurt in order to know pleasure. These two souls found their way back home, despite trial and loss, emptiness and isola-

tion, but even the ocean could not separate what God had written in their hearts. The heart always remembers, my friends, the heart always remembers. Together, they will never be lonely, together they will never be empty, and together, no trial or darkness will ever withstand the power of their light within.

My dearest friends, thank you for allowing me to watch your love story unfold. I have seen some amazing things in my time here on this earth, but I've never seen a love more pure and real as the love you share for each other.

The ocean was the only thing that could be heard as Dr. Pap spoke, besides the sniffles that is. There wasn't a dry eye anywhere. Erika and AJ could hardly speak as they said their vows. They exited the ceremony on horseback after a long kiss, prompted by Dr. Pap's announcement,

"My dearest friends, I am honored to present to you, Drs. Alex and Erika Benjamin."

Erika took a moment to hug Dr. Pap. "Thank you," she said to him, tears falling down her eyes as she was helped onto her horse. She hadn't been called "Dr." in a very long time. She was touched that he slipped a subtle reminder in of who she still was.

The doctors trotted along the beach for a few moments before returning to where they had just taken their vows. They were hugged and kissed by their family and friends. Evie went crazy with pictures, taking over two hundred in just over a half hour. Nearby, the reception tent was being set up. AJ noticed that a stage had been set up on the beach. The couple looked at the kids who had no idea what the elaborate stage was for. They also noticed that Dr. Pap was missing. Instantly, Erika and AJ yelled, "Pap!" still looking at the stage.

The reception was small, intimate, and just perfect for what the couple wanted. Evie sang several songs and her now boyfriend, Joel, facilitated the rest of the music. Erika was happy to see Luke and Jessie dancing nearby, kissing in between talking. Surely, that was a sign of being more than "just friends." Dr. Pap had denied being responsible for anything "sneaky" regarding the stage, and said he thought Evie deserved a stage in which to sing. The couple actually believed him until a familiar song began to play, sung by a familiar voice who had not previously been in attendance.

Dr. Pap arranged for country music star, John Michael Montgomery to be a guest at their reception. He sang, *Hold on to Me,* the first song the couple danced to at the dive bar the first night their relationship turned into what it was always meant to be. When he finished, everyone applauded, and whistling could be heard amongst the guests. The happy couple eagerly ran up to meet the country music star, while lovingly yelling at Dr. Pap for blindsiding them once again. Mr. Montgomery generously agreed to sing a few more of his hit songs, inciting everyone to dance, including many of the Embera children. Dr. Pap managed to score a dance with Gillian, a twenty-two-year-old gymnast who graced him with a quick kiss on the lips at the conclusion of the last song.

Erika and AJ walked along the beach once the party was over. "I never would have imagined all of this," Erika said staring up at the stars.

"I know. It's nothing short of amazing," he agreed.

"And Pap!" Erika exclaimed. "I can't even imagine how much money he spent on all of this!"

"I'm not totally surprised," AJ said thoughtfully. "Pap had a son, but he passed away when he was only five or six. He was born with a rare syndrome. I'd never even heard of it before to be honest."

"Oh my god. I couldn't even imagine. I have goosebumps," she said, rubbing her arms from the chill.

"I know," AJ continued. "So, I think he always kind of looked at me as a son. I know he's loved being my mentor and I've learned a lot from him. I'm a better doctor because of that silly old fool," AJ said laughing, wrapping his arms around his wife and burying his chin into her shoulder. "Kunu, has a few more months, but when he's ready, I'm going to take Pap's advice and do the rotation procedure. He and I will do it together," AJ confirmed.

"I'm glad," Erika said. "I mean, look at Luke," she continued.

"I know, but Kunu is different still, Rik. Kunu is frail. Luke, at least, had been healthy prior to the accident."

"I know, babe, I understand."

"I know you do," he told her. Touching his nose to hers, he said, "I just hope you understand that I'm never letting you go, so you better get used to me as a permanent shadow," he warned.

"I think I can handle that," she said as they made their way home for the night. The couple went to bed, lost thinking about the events of that incredible, picture-perfect day. They were blessed to have shared their day with their friends and loved ones and were overwhelmed by the kindness shown to them by an amazing friend, Dr. Pap. Erika was loving life and couldn't wait for each new day to enjoy hers.

Moving On

While the newlyweds enjoyed their honeymoon, Luke and Jessie were pounding away with training. They trained in four to six hours a day and Luke's hand was getting stronger and stronger. October was approaching quickly and practices at LSU began mid-November. He doubted his hand would be ready to play this spring, and AJ and Dr. Pap concurred. It was a miracle that Luke was able to wrap his hand around a baseball, let alone throw one with any velocity. He had gotten permission to take one online class at LSU in order to keep his foot in the door and his spot on the team. Fortunately, Jessie was well on her way. The Olympic Games didn't begin until late July, which would give her more than enough time, assuming she continued to progress at the same pace. Luke was elated for Jessie and disappointed for himself, but even if he sat at the start of the season, that didn't mean he'd be out the entire season. He wanted to set realistic goals for himself, so he aimed to pitch at least part of one game this season.

Mitch visited many times over the last few months, very impressed by Luke's progress. He, too, never anticipated Luke to be able to throw again, but there he was, increasing in velocity as the months passed. Mitch planned to return just before Christmas so he could celebrate with his son, Jessie, and the rest of the family. Unfortunately, Evie never recovered from the hurtful words Mitch said to her all those months ago. Despite his best efforts of trying to make amends, Evie wanted nothing to do with him. It broke Erika's heart to see this divide in her family, but she knew that if Evie was going to get to a place of forgiveness, she had to get their on her own.

Evie took Erika by surprise when she announced that she'd be leaving Panama with Joel once he was done with PT around the beginning of February. They intended on going back home to Maine, where Joel was originally from, at least in the beginning. Evie enrolled in an online university and would keep herself busy with school when Joel was training for July 2020. Erika pasted on a smile, but she was doubtful of Evie's ability to sustain a relationship and take care of herself completely on her own. Heartbroken, she knew she had to support Evie and let her go.

AJ and Dr. Pap were busy tending to the Embera children and the Olympians. AJ was exceptionally busy with Kunu. He and Dr. Pap agreed that Kunu's surgery would take place right after the New Year. Erika spent her time with the

Embera women, but she began to ache for something more. AJ encouraged her to see what would be involved for her to get her medical license, but that was a road Erika wasn't ready to go down. Before moving to Panama, she thought about petitioning the licensing board and presenting a case to reinstate her license in late 2020, but she'd never once thought about practicing any form of medicine in Panama. Aside from caring for Dr. Pap when he was severely ill around Christmas, she hadn't practiced medicine in close to four years.

The holidays came and went so quickly. AJ and Erika celebrated their first married Christmas together and brought in the New Year with their extended family, the Olympians and the Embera. Erika was collecting all the memories and moments she could with Evie, and Luke, too, for that matter. Both of her babies were preparing to leave in the near future. Evie and Joel planned to leave in four weeks and Luke in four months. Luke was now throwing at 40 mph. It was nowhere close to what he needed to in order to take his place on the mound, but he could see the finish line.

AJ and Dr. Pap prepared for Kunu's surgery. There was one last delay, but this time it was to allow Dr. Pap a few more days to fully recover from the virus that knocked him for a loop. The doctors had their surgical plan down and the room was prepared with everything they needed to heal Kunu. Before Kunu was taken into surgery, the Embera performed a prayer ritual over the young boy and the hands that would fix him. Erika, too, reminded both doctors of how skilled and capable they were, encouraging AJ to have faith in himself. She kissed her husband and even gave Dr. Pap a kiss on the cheek too. She told them it was a kiss for love and luck.

The Unimaginable

Kunu's surgery was very involved. They had one medical assistant, mostly fluent in English, present to help pass surgical equipment and monitor his IV and his vitals. They were two hours into the surgery when Dr. Pap began to tire.

"Hey, Pap, what is it?" AJ asked.

"Nothing, Alex. I'm good, son, just a little tired," he said.

"Pap, I need you here, buddy. Can you make it a little longer?" AJ asked before noticing how badly Dr. Pap was sweating. "Pap, you're sweating through your scrubs, you're soaked," he said.

AJ had never seen this before and he knew something was very wrong. He wondered if Dr. Pap had been really felt better or if he just said he did. The elderly surgeon was anxious to get Kunu's surgery underway, and AJ didn't doubt that Dr. Pap would do or say anything to move it along.

"Ratu," AJ said to the medical assistant, "Go! Hurry! Find Erika and tell her to come now! Hurry, go!" AJ repeated himself. The assistant didn't seem to understand what AJ was asking at first, but then quickly sped out the door to find her.

No sooner did Ratu leave and Kunu's monitors started chiming and beeping. His vitals were dropping, Kunu was crashing.

"What the hell?" AJ said aloud.

Dr. Pap instructed him, "Alex, quickly, check his groin area."

Kunu's groin area was grossly swollen. "Son of a bitch!" AJ yelled.

Kunu flatlined.

"Fuck! Pap, it's a fucking blood clot. I'm starting CPR, charge the paddles."

"Pap," he repeated, "Charge the paddles! Pap!"

Dr. Pap didn't respond. AJ looked down to see him lying on the ground.

"Pap! Pap! No. Don't do this to me! No! Pap I need you. C'mon! Get up, Pap, get up!" AJ screamed in between performing chest compressions on Kunu.

As Erika got closer, she could hear AJ screaming. She burst through the door and the scene was like none she'd ever seen in her life.

"CPR, Rik, CPR, now," AJ yelled.

Erika flew to the ground and checked for a pulse, but Dr. Pap was unresponsive.

"One and two and, three, and four. Breath! Goddamit!" she cried out. "Oh my god! Dr. Pap, Dr. Pap. Oh no, no, no, no, no!" She begged, continuing to do chest compressions.

The sound of flatline rang throughout the room as AJ continued to work on Kunu and Erika on Dr. Pap. It had been forty-five minutes since AJ first began working on Kunu. He did the work of three doctors trying to save Kunu. Erika tried all the lifesaving measures she could but still nothing. Between the shots of epinephrine, CPR, and the paddles, AJ and Erika exhausted all the lifesaving measures they had. Kunu and Dr. Pap were gone.

Erika wondered what the hell happened to that medical assistant, Ratu. She wanted him to come and turn off Kunu's monitor so she didn't have to leave Dr. Pap, but he was nowhere to be found. Erika got up slowly, not wanting to leave her friend's side. She found a clean sheet and laid it over him before turning her attention to AJ, who was still working on Kunu. Erika walked over and turned the monitor off.

"What are you doing?" AJ yelled at her. "Turn that back on, go work on Pap!" He screamed.

"AJ, they're gone. They're gone, AJ, they're both gone."

"No, they're not both gone! Knock it off and put the fucking monitor back on and go help Pap!" He yelled again, even louder than the first.

Erika went over and grabbed AJ. "They are gone! Now, show this boy some respect and stop beating on his poor body, please, AJ!" she begged of him.

AJ stopped. He looked at Erika and fell to his knees crying and screaming, his head buried in her stomach.

"No! Please, God. No!" AJ pleaded. "God bring them back, please, please, please bring them back."

They sat there on the floor next to their friends, two people in which they cared dearly for. Erika felt like she was going to pass out. They both sat there for over an hour, numb and unable to move. Neither knew what in the hell to do next.

"AJ, honey, we have to get Dr. Pap to a city hospital, and we have to tell them about Kunu."

"I can't Erika," he said. "I can't."

"Then you have to let me go so I can. I will send Evie and Luke here to be with you," she told him.

"No, don't. I don't want anybody. I want to be alone with my friends," AJ yelled at her.

"Okay, okay, I'm sorry. I will hurry." Erika promised.

Before she left the surgical room, Erika knelt down next to Dr. Pap. She whispered in his ear as she caressed his forehead.

I'm so sorry, Pap. I love you so much. We all do. You have made so many lives better. You saved my Luke, and in so many ways, you saved my life too. You did good here on this earth, Pap. Now it's time for you to rest. Go be with your son, he's been an angel in heaven, waiting a long time for you to come home. I will do my best to take care of your other son down here on earth. Thank you for showing this stranger so much love. Thank you for taking us to that dive bar and thank you for the lifetime of memories you've given me in less than a year. My heart will never be the same without you.

Erika ran out of the room crying but she had to pull in together. She had to tell Kunu's mother, and she had to tell her children and everyone else about Dr. Pap. She saw Ratu on her way to talk to Kunu's family. He tried to avoid her, but Erika was not about to let that happen.

She caught up to him, flung him around to face her.

"Where were you? We needed your help! We needed your help! Do you understand that?" she yelled.

"I'm Sorry. So Sorry, Ma'am. Scared." He told her.

"Kunu needed you, and Dr. Pap needed you. We all needed your help. So what, you were scared?" she scolded. "I was scared too! Dr. Benjamin was scared! We were all scared, but you didn't even check to see what was going on!" Erika yelled at him again. "You are a disgrace to your tribe, Ratu. A disgrace," she repeated, heartbroken.

"Ms. Erika," Ratu began but was quickly interrupted.

"Don't you dare call me Ms. Erika! That's what Dr. Pap called me," she said, now crying much harder than she had before she saw Ratu. "You don't deserve to do anything similar as that good and gracious man. But what?" she asked him, annoyed with herself that she was still willing to answer his questions.

"What happened to Kunu?" Ratu asked.

"He's dead, Ratu, and so is Dr. Pap," she told him, now beginning to feel herself releasing the anger she felt towards Ratu. "While you were running scared, Dr. Benjamin and I were working, struggling, trying to save those two wonderful people," she informed him. "I need you to help me now, Ratu. I have to tell Kunu's parents and I have no idea how to communicate with them to tell them what has happened." she said.

"Yes, ma'am. I will help. I will follow you," Ratu said.

Kunu's family had been praying when Erika and Ratu approached them. Erika wasn't sure what Ratu said to them upon approaching, but Kunu's mother hugged Erika then she and Kunu's father chanted and circled around her before leaving without saying anything more. Erika had no idea what was happening, but Ratu informed her that is was a gesture of respect since her husband had tried to bring him back from the dead.

Erika was so confused and her mind didn't know which way to go, but she was thankful now for Ratu's help. "Thank you, Ratu. You may call me Ms. Erika if you prefer," she told him, cracking a smile through her tears. "What happens now?" she asked Ratu, "With the body, I mean."

"His parents will take his body from the surgery room, wrap it in Paruma cloth, and present him to the spirits after the family says goodbye," Ratu explained.

"When will they come for his body?" she asked, concerned, thinking of her husband and wondering if he had made any progress in moving from the last position in which she'd left him.

"In whatever amount of time it takes them to gather the villagers they wish to help them honor their son and Dr. Pap too," he said.

"Dr. Pap?" she asked, baffled.

"Yes, Ms. Erika. He was a medicine man and will be given the highest honor there is, Ma'am," Ratu explained.

Erika needed to get back to where AJ was and let him know what was about to happen.

She'd have to talk to Evie and Luke later, they'd have to wait, even if it meant that they heard the horrible news form someone other than her. Ratu agreed to follow her back to the surgical room.

She wanted him there in case the Embera came while she and AJ were still there.

As Erika feared, AJ was still in the same spot in which she'd left him, but now he wouldn't even respond to her.

"AJ, AJ, AJ," she said, her voice growing louder. "AJ, you need to listen to me. Dr. Pap is going to be buried in the village cemetery with Kunu. Kunu's family is on their way now to bring his body back to the village and they are taking Dr. Pap with them too. Ratu told me they will honor him as a medicine man. So, if you want to say goodbye to them privately before the Embera take them and prepare them for burial, you have to do it now," she told him with a tone of urgency in her voice.

AJ didn't move. He was basically catatonic. As she was tending to her husband, she realized she too, hadn't said goodbye to Kunu. Erika lifted herself off the ground from where her husband sat backed up against the wall and basically lifeless. She saw that Kunu's body hadn't been sown up. She didn't want his family to see him in such a gruesome state.

"Ratu, please go find my son and daughter," she instructed him. "Tell them to bring help," Erika added.

She wasn't sure how strong Luke was, and she needed them to help get AJ out of the room and get him back to the compound. This isn't how she wanted them to learn of Dr. Pap's and Kunu's passing but it's what had to be. Erika put on a pair of latex gloves, looked around her for the tools she needed and began sewing up the sweet young boy laid before her. She noticed that he had a smile on his face. Tears filled Erika's eyes as she worked. She paused for a second to think how he must have just made a layup, playing basketball with the angels and a sense of peace came across her.

Luke and Jessie entered the room first, next came Evie with Joel. Together with Ratu, they lifted AJ, first to his knees and then up onto his feet but he wouldn't walk and he wouldn't speak.

Evie watched her mother sew up the young boy. She had never seen her mother in such a capacity. She was impressed at the wrong time, she felt, but impressed, nonetheless. Evie was proud of how her mother took control, instead of falling apart, and did what was necessary. Evie knew this would be a moment she'd one day look back on. If she felt like something was too much for her to handle, she'd envision the strength her mother demonstrated that day and push forward.

"Are you okay, Mom?" Evie asked. Erika managed to crack a smile at Evie to assure her that she was fine.

"Yes, sweetie, I'm okay. I just need you all to please take AJ home and lay him in bed. Stay with him, please?" she asked. "I will get there as soon as I can and explain everything," she promised.

Everyone agreed. They helped AJ out of the room, crying and trying to process what they'd just seen. Erika was just finishing up with Kunu when she heard the Embera. She kissed Kunu on the head and covered him with a white sheet before stepping aside. The Embera entered and four tall men tended to Dr. Pap while Kunu's parents and kin tended to him. They left rather quickly, leaving Erika alone in the surgical room, speechless, and able to hear only the chanting of the Embera as it faded into the distance. Erika's hands shook as she removed her gloves and she looked around at the room, feeling complete emptiness. She washed her hands, catching a glimpse of herself in the mirror above the sink. She was covered in blood. It hadn't even occurred to her to cover herself with more than just latex gloves. Erika sat down in a lone chair in the corner of the room. She buried her head in her hands and sobbed.

Once Erika was able to compose herself, she headed back home where the kids waited.

Ratu was still there and had filled them in on what he knew prior to Erika returning home.

"Ms. Erika," Ratu began. "I will leave now to go clean the surgery room. I don't want Dr. Benjamin to see sadness when he returns," Ratu explained.

Erika was grateful. She thanked him and apologized for her anger towards him earlier that afternoon.

"Mom, what happened?" Evie asked.

Erika looked around at the sad faces, Luke and Joel looking off to the side and Jessie and Evie noticeably crying. Erika tried to explain what had happened the best she could and everyone listened as she spoke.

"Ratu came running for me and told me that AJ needed me to come right away. The only thing I knew at that time was that Dr. Pap was tired and had been sweating," she said. "I figured they needed me to help out so he could take a break. I had no idea what was going on. The closer I got I could hear AJ screaming. I ran in and saw AJ working on Kunu, trying to get his heart started. His monitor was going off, everything was chiming and beeping, and all I heard was the sound of his flatline on the monitor," she told them solemnly. "Dr. Pap was unresponsive and lying on the floor when I got there. I couldn't find a pulse. I did CPR, I injected him with epinephrine, and I used the paddles but nothing," Erika continued.

"AJ did the same for Kunu. We just couldn't bring them back. We just couldn't bring them back. I don't know for sure, obviously, but I think Dr. Pap had a heart attack. He had been really sick. We thought it was the flu, but I'm guessing the virus went to his heart. Myocarditis presents like the flu. There's no way we could have known, especially since it seemed like Dr. Pap was getting better," she explained. "Sweet Kunu, I really can't be sure at all. He was so sick. It took so many months for him to even be able to sustain this surgery, and I think he would have but it looks like he had a blood clot. When I was closing him up, I saw a lot of swelling, an abnormal amount, around his groin area. That's the only thing that would explain him crashing so quickly, especially given the area of his surgery."

"Oh my god, Mom," Luke finally spoke. "This is unreal. What happened to AJ?" Luke asked.

"I think he's in shock. He just watched two people he loved very dearly die, and he wasn't able to save them," Erika explained to them. "AJ is going to take this very hard for a very long time, so we need to support him," she instructed everyone. "Can you guys give me a little time with AJ now? I want to clean him up and try getting him to talk," Erika told them. "Please go back to the village and see if you can somehow find out when the burial will be. I should have asked Ratu when he was here," she said.

"Of course, Mom, we will be back in a bit," Luke promised, leading the four of them out the door.

Broken Again

Erika went to their bedroom where the kids had brought AJ a short while before. He was still in his scrubs, covered in Kunu's blood. He wasn't sleeping but he wasn't awake either.

"C'mon, AJ, let's get you out of these scrubs, honey," she tried to coax him.

After a long struggle, Erika was able to get his scrubs off and she got him into the shower. When the water hit him, AJ immediately came to.

"Erika! They're gone. They're gone," AJ repeated.

"I know, baby, I know."

Erika climbed into the shower, knelt down beside where he was crouched, and rocked him in her arms, singing to him, softly. She would have stayed in that corner of the shower with him all day if it would have helped him. The water ran down their bodies, cleansing them but Erika didn't know from what. Erika knew they both needed to be in there together, trying to let some of their hurt out, so the new hurt could fill their hearts tomorrow.

Erika knew her life had changed once again, but this type of change was worse than the unknown. Their lives were consumed by pain and grief. She doubted her husband would ever be able to recover from it and live life with the same happy heart he'd had up until then. Erika recalled her conversation with Dr. Pap and his warning that some doctors never recover from a loss as great as what they just experienced. Erika promised AJ she'd be his rock. She'd do whatever she could to help him, regardless of what that meant for her, regardless if she had to put her own hurt and her own heart aside to help make him better.

Once the water turned cold, Erika helped AJ stand up and then they went to bed. AJ didn't speak at all that night, and she didn't push him. He would talk when he was ready. They stared up at the ceiling, AJ often forgetting to blink and Erika blinking so rapidly, trying to clear the waterfall from her eyes. Eventually, they both fell asleep.

With the morning came, the realization of what transpired the day before, along with the stabbing pain that went with it. Evie let Erika know that the burial was going to be at sundown that night. Dr. Pap and Kunu would be laid out that afternoon at 1:00 p.m. for visitation until it was time for their burial ceremony. Erika relayed the information to AJ and was surprised at the response she got.

"I'm not going, Erika." he said.

"What do you mean you're not going?" she asked, repeating what she thought she just heard. "This is the last chance you'll have to say goodbye to your dearest friend and Kunu. Kunu loved you, baby. Please, say goodbye to them. It's wrong not to," she told him, never expecting what came next.

"Then I guess you should add it to the fucking list of shit I've done wrong this week, okay? Erika, I'm so sorry that I don't fall under your definition of what is appropriate," AJ yelled at her.

Erika literally threw up in her mouth, she felt sickened by what AJ just said to her and with such a degree of contempt towards her in his voice. She had never heard him so angry, and especially at her.

"AJ!"

"What, Erika, what?"

"I know you're hurting but yelling at me and losing your mind right now is not going to bring them back. Things will only get worse if—"

AJ didn't allow her to finish.

"Yes, Erika, I've lost my mind. Sure, that's it, because losing my mind is such a better choice than trying to understand that maybe I just don't have the strength to go. I'm sorry I'm not you, Erika. I wasn't able to swoop in and save the day for the people I love, like you. I saved everyone but the people I love. But you, you have me all figured out, don't you? The great Dr. Erika Doss, the great psychiatrist gone rogue."

"AJ, stop! Please," she begged him, her blood having drained from her body and her heart completely broken. Erika silently prayed she could wake up from this nightmare.

"I'm sorry, Erika. Did I hurt your feelings? God forbid I hurt your goddamn feelings. You're right, I'm wrong, so I think I will leave now so I don't disappoint you or hurt your feelings. Okay, Erika? Just leave me the hell alone. I don't care what you think or what you have to say about anything right now. I just want to think about them and not you for once. Is that okay, Erika? Is that okay if you're not the only thing on my mind just for today?" he screamed.

AJ left, angry, slamming the door behind him, not even giving a second glance back at his broken bride. Erika couldn't move. She couldn't feel her body except for her tears. When she finally did move, she climbed back into bed and continued to cry. She stretched out her arm out across AJ's side of the bed and brought his pillow to her face. She could smell him and her heart broke even more. She didn't know what to do, and it was obvious he didn't want her to do anything.

Erika mustered the strength to get up, her eyes swollen from hours of crying and a headache that pounded so badly, she could feel throbbing in her eye. She wondered if she'd see AJ at the visitation. She knew AJ would regret it if he stayed away and not said his final goodbye.

It was almost 9:00 p.m. before everyone had a chance to pay their respects to Kunu and their medicine man, Dr.

Pap. Embera, old and young came from many villages from Panama to Colombia to say goodbye. All the Olympians who were still staying at the compound were in attendance as well. Erika went to sit next to her children as the burial ceremony began. She received a lot of questions regarding AJ's whereabouts and why he wasn't there. Erika told them he wasn't coping well and asked that they remember him in their prayers. She prayed he might still show up.

It wasn't until halfway through the ceremony that Erika caught a glimpse of AJ standing far away in the distance. She doubted he could hear the ceremony from where he was but was glad that he was there, nonetheless. After the ceremony, Erika had a chance to walk with Evie.

She explained AJ's behavior and she, too, was at a loss.

"Don't let him get to you, Mom. He's hurting," Evie told her.

"We are all hurting, Eves," Erika countered.

"Yes, we're all hurting, but not like him and you know that," the wise youth reminded her mother.

"I understand what you're saying. It was just as if someone had stabbed me in the heart. I had never been talked to by anyone like that, and he was the last one I'd expect it from," she told her.

"I have," Evie reminded her, referring to when Mitch blamed her for Luke's accident.

Erika thought about Mitch's emotional state at that point in time and considered that AJ, too, would come around in time and realize he was wrong to treat her like that.

"Mom, I'm going to walk you back and then you're going to go talk to your husband," Evie told her. Erika nodded in agreement.

Erika beat AJ home and she wasn't sure if she was relieved or upset that he wasn't there. It had been yet another long, emotional day and Erika was about to go to bed when AJ came home.

"Hey, Aej," Erika began. "How are you?" she asked.

"I've had better days," he responded, not looking at her.

I saw you at the burial ceremony. I was glad you came, even if you were off in the distance, Dr. Pap and Kunu knew you were there," Erika reassured him.

"I couldn't face everyone," he said. "I didn't deserve to be in the same room with all those wonderful people who counted on me. I didn't just kill a son of theirs, I killed their medicine man, their doctor too," AJ said, beginning to cry once again.

Erika went to hug her husband but was quickly rejected.

"Please, Erika, please don't touch me right now. I can't even look at you, I'm sorry, I just can't," he said, slightly looking in her direction but doing everything he could to avoid eye contact with her.

"AJ, please tell me why you're so angry with me," she begged. "I tried to help. I tried to save him, just like you tried to save Kunu. We did our best, both of us. I really don't understand why you're acting this way, but you're breaking my heart," she pleaded with him.

"You really don't know why I'm so angry with you? Really Erika?"

"Yes, really, AJ, I don't have a clue, and since when do you call me Erika?" she asked now beginning to feel a mix of anger with hurt.

"Pap and Kunu are dead because of you," he said, with complete seriousness.

Erika's knees were going to give out on her any second. She sat on the bed and looked at her husband through her tear-stained eyes. She tried to catch her breath and speak but nothing came out.

"You told me to do that procedure on Kunu. You did. You knew I didn't want to but you pushed me into it, bringing Pap into it, too, telling me to work with him, to do it together," AJ reminded her with malice. "So I did, Erika. I did, but your idea, your mission, killed them both, *together*. So congrats, you won and the rest of us lost."

Erika couldn't process what was happening with her husband. She went to the closet for her suitcase and began packing her things.

"Actually, Erika, I think that's a good idea. I think you should leave," AJ said without any doubt in his voice. "Luke's doing well here, I hope you still let him stay until April," he continued. "I think we may have made a mistake, Erika, and I'm sorry for that. I guess our story was too good to be true after all."

Erika took off her wedding ring and tossed it on the dresser. She's almost finished packing by the time AJ finished telling her how horrible she was and that everything they had was a mistake.

"AJ," she began, "Let me fill you in on a little secret that you never knew. When we first got here, Dr. Pap pulled me aside and asked me to see if I could get you to consider that rotation procedure or whatever he called it," Erika said.

AJ listened, but decided he wasn't going to believe anything she had to say.

"It was the first time I had ever seen you with Kunu," she explained. "Dr. Pap said that you're a good doctor but that it's not until you stop playing it safe that you'll be a great doctor. He said that you need to trust yourself and your abilities, and until you fail one day, you will never really rise. He was afraid that the one time you failed, you'd act just like this," Erika told him. "It's ironic, too, because I specifically told Pap that I would encourage you based on my faith in you and that I'd never tell you what to do," Erika insisted, shaking her head in disbelief at how the exact thing she had wanted to avoid ended up happening anyway.

AJ started to soften as she spoke, feeling slightly guilty for his behavior. He turned away from her when she tried one final attempt to reach out for his hand. AJ's head and heart just ached. He knew what he was doing was wrong but he was angry at her and he didn't know what to do with this feeling that he'd never experienced towards her before.

Erika gathered her things, and on her way out the door she told him, "If you want to blame me for their deaths, if that's what you need to do so you don't have to face your own demons, AJ, then be my guest," she said. "With all the mistakes I have made in my life, I know that a clot took Kunu and a heart attack took Dr. Pap. I know that those are two things that I had no way of knowing or controlling," Erika told him.

AJ wanted to reach out and take her in his arms but he wouldn't allow himself to. AJ needed a wall between them to alleviate his pain, and it was easier to blame her than to work through his own self-doubt. AJ knew that Dr. Pap suspected that Kunu might have a blood clot. It was one of the things they feared could happen and apparently did. He and Dr. Pap never really addressed how to prevent the clot from occurring. They assumed with his increased movement and activity, the odds of a clot occurring were minimal.

"I'm leaving so you'll have what you want, but this isn't about me, it's about you. You run, you play it safe, and you try to childproof your life," Erika told him. "You can have the best of everything here, AJ, but if you're broken, then none of these matter. Until you accept that you're human and not perfect, and until you accept that sometimes sad things happen, then you're never going to have a life," Erika said, walking out the door. "Bye, Aej."

Erika sped-walked to Evie's. She had never moved that fast, carrying all that she had, crying at the same time. Erika could hardly see in front of her. She was going to spend one night at Evie's and head home to Michigan in the morning. She prayed she's be able to find an early flight.

Luke came over to Evie's after Erika told him she'd be leaving in the morning.

"I just can't believe that all of this is happening," he said. "Mom, why don't you just stay here at Evie's for a couple days. Don't leave yet. Maybe he'll come around."

"Luke, it's okay," Erika told him. "You stay," she said. "Even AJ said you should stay and finish out your therapy. You've come so far and you're almost there, so you do you, and I will be at your first game," she promised him, offering him the best smile she could muster at the moment.

"I'm going to go with you, Mom," Evie said. "I was planning on heading back to the States with Joel anyway in another week or so. I will go home with you and then meet him in Maine, but I don't want you to be alone," Evie stated, making it very clear to Erika that her decision had been made.

"Thanks, Evie. Thanks both of you. I love you guys so much," she said hugging them.

By the grace of God, Erika found an early flight and they departed Panama at 8:05 a.m. on a one-way flight back to Michigan. Erika knew that the days ahead of her would be awful. She'd had broken hearts before but nothing like this. Never before had she gone from such happiness to the lowest depths of hell and depression. Erika hated inconveniencing Evie, but she was glad Evie wad going home with her.

It was very early, but Erika and Evie said goodbye to as many of their friends at the compound and the Embera Village as they could. She was given a goodbye blessing by the Embera, who didn't understand why she and Evie were leaving so quickly.

Erika walked past the villa she shared with AJ and where Luke had spent the majority of his time healing. She was grateful for what AJ had done for her son. For that reason alone, she didn't regret the months she had with him in Panama. AJ broke her heart and hurt her very badly, but Erika knew she'd remain in love with him for the rest of her life. He was a part of her soul, and she'd have to find a way to live without him, but he wasn't anyone her heart could forget. Erika spent much of the flight home with her head on Evie's shoulder. She needed the comfort. She thought about the condo she'd left behind and realized it had probably been sold or rented out by now. Fortunately, Erika only had to panic for a moment, until Evie told her AJ had paid the remainder of the lease because he knew she'd been worried about the worst-case scenario.

Michigan was just the same as when she'd left. It was almost February now and there was at least a foot of snow on the ground. It was a far cry from the 90s she'd grown accustomed to in Panama. The condo was the same bland condo. She was glad she remembered to pick up her belongings from storage on the way home from the airport. When she woke up in Michigan the next morning, she heard the birds chirping, offering hope in the day to come, much like they had in the early mornings just before her fairytale began. As she looked around her room, she thought of the last time she had been there, whipping around, packing everything up, excited, jubilant, and grateful. The past nine months had been quite the whirlwind, and she was trying to look at her time with AJ and all the time she spent in Panama with her many new friends in a positive light. It was just very hard to get past her broken heart.

Evie, Mitch, and some of Erika's other friends thought she would have heard from AJ right away, possibly even a day or two after she'd left, but Erika knew better. She had come to see how poorly he reacted to failure or things working out differently than he predicted. She wondered if she'd ever hear from him again and began looking into a divorce. Erika was angry at herself for letting him in, but she had trusted him, and he was always wonderful to her when they were in school together. She allowed herself to form a false sense of security with him.

Whenever she spoke with Luke, she refused to talk or ask about AJ. In fact, it had been two months since either of them said his name. Neither wanted to be the first to bring him up. When it became time for Luke to return home, focused on his spring semester, and the potential to play in at least one baseball game at LSU, AJ's name finally rose to the surface. Erika knew that Luke's progress had been remarkable, still she needed to know that he was really ready.

"Does AJ think you're ready?" Erika asked.

"Mom, I didn't know if I should mention him but, honestly, he hasn't been here. In fact, I saw him once just three days ago and, had I not been so pissed at him, I probably would have cared enough to ask if he was okay." Luke said. "Some other doc, Dr. Roman, has been here working with Jessie and I and a few of the other Olympians, but Jessie and I are basically the last ones left," Luke continued. "The compound is a ghost town. I don't know what he's doing, but nobody new has started here since you left," Luke informed her. "But I have to tell you that in the couple of hours he was here, he worked really hard to find Jessie and me. He asked if I knew where you were staying and if you'd gone back to Michigan," Luke explained.

Erika felt her heart jump for a moment before reminding herself she'd be a fool to give him the time of day. "What did you say?" Erika asked.

"I told him that he had your number and if he wanted information, he'd have to ask you himself." Luke held his breath waiting for his mother's reaction, hoping he hadn't messed anything up.

"Great. That was perfect, Luke. Thanks for having my back, honey," Erika replied.

"Phew! Good! I was worried I said the wrong thing," he laughed.

Returning to her original question, "Does this Dr. Roman feel like you're ready to fast-pitch?" she asked.

"Yeah, I'm throwing wicked hard, a 64 mph fast-pitch, my highest speed yet!"

"No, what?" Erika asked. "Honey, that can't be. You were only pitching 59-60 mph before the accident," she said.

"I know! Doc Roman said it's some funny springy tendon thing. I don't know, and I don't care. I'm just going with it!" Luke said, feeling confident.

"I can't wait until you're back and I get to sit in the stands, cheering you on again," Erika told him, feeling very proud of everything he's overcome.

Erika was really curious about what was going on with AJ. As much as she tried to not care, she was worried if he was okay and hoped he wasn't having a mental breakdown, well, not any more than he already had. Admittedly, she felt better that he still cared enough for her to ask about her. Maybe everything they shared wasn't a lie after all.

Erika had been in a trance when she was interrupted by her phone. April was here and real estate was once again back in business. After her call had ended, Erika reminded herself that she had to stay focused. She let AJ get in her head once and she turned her life upside down. She wasn't about to let him do it again all because he simply asked her son if she'd returned to Michigan.

━⁓∽◦◯⥈◯⥇◯∽◦⁓━

April came and went. Luke returned to Michigan for a brief second before heading to LSU. Jessie returned to her team and was looking forward to leaving for Tokyo in another month. Luke planned on joining her in Tokyo once his season ended. He and Evie made arrangements to live together for the six weeks they were in Tokyo supporting Joel and Jessie. Erika stayed busy, she decided it was time to paint the condo. She was tired of bland and sad. After all, her life was not bad, and she had AJ and Dr. Pap to thank for that. Both of her children found a significant other, Luke made a miraculous recovery and Evie had lived the life of a princess. She felt things she never knew were even possible.

Erika thought a lot about Dr. Pap. It wasn't until his death that she really thought about the type of person he was. He had lost his son, his wife left him after their son passed, and instead of feeling sorry for himself, he decided to make the world a better place. Her replaced his own loneliness with humor and he lived. He lived the life God had given him to the fullest, and Erika was determined to do the same. Plus, in another week, everyone would be together again for Luke's comeback game. Luke called Erika a few days before and let her know that he'd be the starting pitcher against Florida State. Evie, Joel, and Jessie planned to meet up with Erika and Mitch the night before the game in Louisiana. Erika was happy to learn that Ump Ted planned on attending Luke's comeback game as well. He, Mitch, and Erika had actually become good friends since Erika returned from Panama.

Mitch had been very supportive of Erika since she returned with her broken heart. He even eventually realized that AJ was the guy she'd been friends with back in med school when they first started dating. Erika and Mitch got a good laugh out of how clueless Mitch could be. Evie eventually accepted Mitch's apology, and they had a few conversations over the phone since. They planned to meet for lunch, just the two of them, before she headed to Tokyo to watch Joel in the Olympics. Erika wished Dr. Pap could be there for Luke's game. She knew, though, that he'd be there in spirit. Secretly, she wanted AJ to be there too, but tried to push her continual thoughts of him out of her head.

LSU and a Bear

Erika was amazed at how packed the LSU stadium was, but she seemed to be the only one who was shocked.

"You're kidding, right?" Evie asked "Mom, its LSU versus Florida State, seriously," she continued, eye roll and all.

The game was spectacular. Luke struggled the first two innings. He had the speed but couldn't find the spot. Ump Ted tried to call his pitches from the stands and ironically did a better job from the stands than he had the game on the ill-fated day. By the bottom of the third, he was killing the opposition. Luke had three strike outs in a row, and he was on hyperdrive. The game ended in an LSU victory, 12-8, and Luke was interviewed after the game.

Erika stood by waiting for Luke to finish the interview so she could hug her amazing son.

"I have two men in particular, Dr. Peta Altman-Panu, or Dr. Pap as we called him, and Dr. Alex Benjamin to thank for my being here today," Luke told the reporters. "I was originally told I'd may never walk again or even be able to keep my hand, let alone be throwing 60 mph baseballs. Those two docs were my orthopedic surgeons and my friends. They offered me an opportunity to receive the best physical therapy and partnered me with the best trainers in the world, not just the country, and that made the difference. Without them, I really wouldn't be here right now," he admitted. "Dr. Pap passed away a few months ago, but I needed to throw his name out as someone who changed my life forever. I also have to thank my mom. She took a chance for me that allowed me access to everyone and everything I needed to make this day possible, so thanks, Mom, for being willing to turn your world upside down for me," he said, looking directly at Erika.

She smiled and then turned away, needing a moment to collect herself.

Erika was about to search for the rest of her family amongst the mass amount of people trying to exit the stadium when she heard him.

"That was quite the interview," came from a voice Erika would know anywhere. She paused, took a breath, and turned around to see AJ standing in front of her. He had almost gotten plowed over by what looked to be a family of summa wrestlers, before stepping to the side to avoid being trampled. Erika just stared, this time in somewhat of a catatonic state herself.

"You saw the game?" she asked.

"Yeah, of course," he said smiling.

Erika hadn't seen that smile since before Dr. Pap and Kunu died. It still made her heart melt.

"How are you?" he asked, wondering how long she'd allow him to talk to her before punching him in the face.

"I'm good, AJ, I'm actually really good." Erika told him. "Well, thank you, for coming to the game and for everything you've done for Luke. Truly, we are both beyond grateful," she said.

Out of the corner of her eye, she saw Mitch and the kids waiting at the top of the stairs for her. Mitch tried to quickly move everyone out of her view so Erika might be more willing to spend some talking to AJ, but it didn't work.

"AJ, I gotta go," she told him. "They're waiting for me at the top of the stairs," she told him, trying to maneuver her way past him.

"Wait. Please," AJ asked. "Can we talk? If not now, then meet me for breakfast, lunch, dinner, a drink, I don't care, I just want to talk to you," he told her.

"Talk to me? I wanted to talk to you then, in Panama, before and even after you told me our marriage was a mistake. I wanted to talk to you the first week I had left, or hell, even the second. It's been *four* months, AJ, and now you want to talk?" she said angrily.

"I know, Rik, I know—"

Erika quickly interrupted. "Oh, so now I'm Rik again. I see how it is," she said. "Well, Alex, no. I don't want to talk to you. Goodbye, Alex," she said as she walked past him. "Thank you for coming out for Luke," she told him, refusing to look back.

Erika was met with a slew of "Are you okay?" from everyone. Mitch, Luke, Jessie, and Joel, all wanted to hear what AJ had to say.

"He asked if I'd meet him to talk," Erika told everyone.

"And…," they all said, almost perfectly in sync.

"I said no. What do you think I said?" Erika looked at them, shocked that they even had to ask.

Mitch's response, of all people surprised her the most. "Why?" Mitch asked.

"Why?" Erika repeated. "Oh, let's see. First, he placed blame on me for Dr. Pap's and Kunu's death. Did he forget that I was the one who did CPR on Pap then stitched Kunu up after having to tell his family about his death? Oh, and then, he proceeded to tell me how our marriage was a mistake and that it was a good idea that I left. All of that, to be followed by four months, *four months,* Mitch, of *zero,* and I mean *zero* contact," Erika exploded at him.

On that note, the kids decided to go for a walk. "Just text us when you're done killing dad," Luke told her, somewhat truthfully.

"Erika," Mitch began. "You're a tough person. You just are. You also have the ability to overcome, to get back up again, and to say, 'fuck you' to the world with confidence, but you weren't like that when I first met you," he said. "You worried about everything and everyone. You worried what people thought, you had to make everyone happy but yourself, that is, and it wasn't until hardship hit that you grew your thick skin," he continued.

"I never blamed you for somebody dying or told you that our marriage was a mistake or disappeared from your life for four months," Erika fought back.

"Uhhh, Erika, you told me our marriage was a mistake on a daily basis. You went weeks without talking to me. I don't know what's worse, having someone you had to see every day ignore you and the helplessness you feel when you just can't reach them or having someone removed from your life. I don't know, Erika, but I tend to think it's easier not having a constant, every day in-your-face reminder of someone you want to be with so badly, but they don't really want you, at least not anymore," he confessed. Then he continued, "You never blamed me for anyone's death, but you told me many times that if you 'offed yourself,' it would be my fault and that you hoped me and my 'asshole' kids would die in a burning building," Mitch reminded her, somewhat laughing now at the memory of the craziness that defined their life back then.

Erika couldn't help but laugh too. "I remember," she admitted. "Those were insane times," she said. "Everything was so extreme and emotional back then. I know I didn't handle it well," Erika confessed. "I'm not like that anymore though," she declared, waiting for Mitch to agree with her.

Mitch sat down next to her on the bench. "Did you hear what you just said?" he asked her.

Erika looked at him, confused at first. "Wait, no, it's not the same situation," she began before being cut off by Mitch.

"Don't tell me it's not the same…oh and isn't that what AJ said when you compared Luke's procedure to what needed to be done with Kunu, and you wouldn't accept that response from him?" Mitch jabbed at her.

"Mitch, I appreciate what you're trying to do, and I get that you're trying to help me, albeit weird since you're my ex, but—" Erika tried to explain before Mitch cut her off once again.

"Erika, I can't think of anything more emotional than losing a father-figure and someone you loved as a son in the same day, let alone within the same ten-minute period. When you said nasty things to me, I had to take it for what it was— your way of coping—and I was the person closest to you, so it was my job to have the thick skin. You're right, you don't react the same way to things as you did back then and neither will AJ. I just think that you might want to consider trying on a thick skin for him this time. I've known everything there is to know about you, Erika, everything. We weren't good as husband and wife, but we make really good friends," he told her.

Mitch was right, and he'd won. Erika softened and listened now to what he had to say.

"I know the past few months have been hard. I know he hurt you. I also know that you're still in love with him and he with you. You will regret it if you don't talk to him, Erika," he concluded.

Erika paused and then wrapped her arms around Mitch's neck.

"I'm really lucky to have you in my life, Mitch," she told him, feeling appreciative of his candidness and honesty. "I'll call him later. I will talk with him," she said.

"Actually"—Mitch said, as he started to move away from her in anticipation that what he said next would cause her to really punch him in the face—"I texted him and told him to wait for you. He's at 'D' Gate, at the north end of the parking lot. I will take the kids back to the hotel and catch up with you later." Mitch walked quickly down the stadium corridor away from Erika.

"Mitch, you might want to sleep with one eye open from now on! I swear, it's on," she yelled, hoping it was loud enough that he heard. Secretly, she was really happy Mitch had done that.

As Erika walked to "D" Gate, she wondered what she should say to him first. She really didn't need to worry about that though because AJ had it covered. Erika walked to the north end and immediately saw AJ standing outside of a black

Land Rover, his most recent rental she presumed. When she got to where he was standing, Erika started to explain that Mitch talked her into coming down, but he stopped her with a long kiss she hadn't anticipated and a yearning for more that she hadn't expected.

"I went home to Colorado for a bit before heading down here," he began. "I received your divorce summons, but I burned it in my fire pit," he told her. Erika noticed he was still wearing his ring. He caught her looking at his hand, and told her, "I've never taken it off, Rik, not once. Not even to shower, shit, and shave," he said, earning a smile and an eye roll from her.

"AJ," she began, "I understand that you were in the worst state of mind that a person can be in, but I don't know how to let go of the hurt I feel. I don't know how to let go of the betrayal I feel. I don't know how to heal from this," she confessed. "Once again, I had to re-invent my life, find some resemblance of a life again without you. My heart ached every day," she admitted.

"Mine did, too, Rik. Maybe I should have contacted you sooner, but I didn't want to mess things up even more," AJ explained. "I actually called for a flight the morning you left, but I knew I needed to get my head straight. I wondered if every plane that flew above the compound that morning was yours," he admitted. "I'm not running the compound anymore," he told her. "I spent almost two months just wandering. I needed to clear my heard and I needed to understand myself better. When I said those horrible things to you, I knew I was wrong, but I didn't know what to do with everything I felt. Everything you said when you were leaving was true, and I knew it. I just didn't know what to do about it, Rik, I was so lost and scared. I wasn't sure I could make it in medicine without Pap," he told her, now wearing his heart on a sleeve in a way Erika had never seen Dr. Benjamin do.

Changing the topic from himself, he redirected their conversation back to his work. "I don't know if you heard, but I hired a replacement and I said goodbye to the Embera. We stopped taking Olympians, too, until Dr. Roman can hire and train at least three more docs to assist him," AJ continued, spelling out his plans. "I might be back one day, but for now I just signed on as a partner in a huge medical practice in Colorado."

Erika looked up when she heard what he had done, sensing her potential disapproval, he added, "That being said, I would follow *you* this time anywhere you want, if you'd give me another chance. I would honestly go anywhere to be with you," he declared.

"My head is spinning, Aej," Erika told him. "I don't know what you expect me to do, AJ, I really don't. I need some time, please. Can I have some time to really process everything?" she asked. "I mean, as of two hours ago, I hadn't seen nor heard from you in four months, and even though I understand that you needed to clear your head, you need to allow me to do the same," she said as a matter of fact.

"I understand, Rik," AJ assured her.

"You're probably going to be mad at me, but I took a chance and bet on having an opportunity today," he told her, smirking.

"What, AJ? What?" Erika repeated feeling overwhelmed already. He reached in the back of the truck, turning for a moment to ask her if she was ready.

"At least I'm not blindfolded this time," she said jokingly, a comment that brought a smile to AJ's face.

Before AJ was able to show her his surprise, she heard the sweetest, baby bark she'd ever heard. Erika gasped and covered her mouth.

"I thought he could keep you company if you ever get lonely," AJ told her. "I know it's gotta be different now that the kids are gone," AJ said as he handed her a handsome eight-week-old chocolate lab puppy with the brightest blue eyes.

"Oh my god!" Erika kept repeating as she embraced the puppy and he pelted her face with kisses. "He's the cutest thing I've ever seen," she told him.

"Hey!" AJ challenged her.

"You know what I mean!" she said laughing, taking in the smell of puppy breath and enjoying his sweet kisses. Erika took a better look at the blue bow tie around her new puppy's neck. She began to cry realizing that it was her wedding band.

"Please wear it," AJ asked. "At least until you are a hundred percent sure that you either can't or don't want to be with me anymore," he said, continuing to pull on her heartstrings.

Erika took her ring from the bow tie and AJ asked if he could return her ring to its proper place.

"May I?"

"Sure," she said, holding out her hand for him as she had another time before, wiping a few tears away.

"I love you, Rik. I really love you," AJ told her, this time looking right into her eyes.

Sniffling, "I love you, too. God, I love you, it's just been so hard," she told him now crying much harder than before.

"I know, sweetie, I know and I'm so sorry. I will spend the rest of my life trying to make it up to you if you let me," he promised, squishing the chocolate lab puppy as he embraced her and kissed her for as long as she'd let him.

They held each other until they were interrupted by puppy bark.

"Why don't you figure out what you're going to name him as I drive you back to your hotel? That way, Mitch won't have to come all the way back to get you," AJ suggested.

"Okay, yeah. Thanks. I'm sure he'd appreciate that," Erika said, hardly acknowledging AJ at this point, completely focused on her new puppy-friend.

"Crap," Erika said, "I hope the hotel is dog friendly, and I will have to get a crate for him for the flight home," she continued, thinking aloud. "Actually, you're all set. I may have talked to Mitch and made sure about the hotel and the crate is already waiting for you in your room," AJ assured her.

When they arrived back at her hotel, Erika thanked him again and promised to call him when she was back in Michigan.

"So, what did you decide you were going to name the little guy?" AJ asked.

"Bear," she said. "My Maxie always reminded me of a big brown bear, so I said if I ever had another chocolate lab, his name would be Bear," she explained, smiling.

"Bear it is," AJ confirmed.

Erika walked around his Land Rover, Bear snuggled in her arms, and gave AJ a final kiss through the window.

"Thank you," he said, touching her hand, and looking where the ring had been returned to its proper place.

"Goodnight, Aej," she called back to him as she walked into her hotel.

A New Month

Erika couldn't wait to get home with her new puppy, and she thought a lot about AJ, fiddling with her wedding ring. She knew that she didn't want their marriage to be over, and she knew she wouldn't be able to stay away from him, so she chose not to fight it. She decided that he wanted to spend some time with her, both in Michigan and Colorado. She also had a request for him and his response would give her a strong indication of where his mindset was. With Luke and Evie heading to Tokyo in a couple weeks, she'd be free from any kids dropping in and would be able to focus her attention on AJ and their marriage. Erika took a day to love on Bear and to enroll him in puppy boot camp, so he'd stop pooping on the floor. She remembered when Max went through that puppy poo-poo stage and she wanted to be more proactive this time. Erika was in love with Bear and he loved being her shadow.

Erika kept her promise and called AJ. They talked for hours the first couple nights, getting to know each other all over again. They arranged for him to spend a week with her in Michigan and then she and Bear would stay a week with him in Colorado. AJ decided to wait another month before starting his new position, so he too could dedicate the time to him and Erika. Erika remembered the blissful feelings she had with him, and little by little, her hurt melted away. Over the two weeks they spent together, they reconnected whole-heartedly, body and soul. Erika knew she wanted to stay with him but before she became any further re-invested, she needed to know where he was emotionally.

When their week in Colorado was coming to an end, AJ wondered where they would go from here. He agreed that the past two weeks had been amazing and that he, too, felt alive again. They had planned for two weeks, but Erika had asked if he could set aside a month. He didn't want to push her by asking, but he had no idea what to expect next. Finally, the day before she and Bear were scheduled to return to Michigan, Erika hit him with the first half of her question.

"So, do you still have two more weeks available if we were to go somewhere for a short visit?"

Relieved that he would have more time together, he was eager to offer her anywhere she wanted to go.

"What do you think about going back to Panama for a couple weeks? I'd like to visit the Embera and for whatever reason, I feel the need to reconnect with you in Panama," she explained.

Without hesitation, AJ reached out for her hand. "Definitely, I would love to do that," he told her, smiling, as was she.

"Do you think you might want to talk about the rest of our lives *together* while we're there, like where you'd like to live together as a couple, married, and waking up next to each other every morning?" he asked, holding his breath until she responded.

"Yeah, I would really like to have that talk with you," Erika said, feeling certain. "There's one more thing I'd like to do with you, AJ," she told him, sprouting the second half of her two-part quest. Erika took a deep breath. "I would like you come with me and visit Dr. Pap and Kunu where they're buried," she asked, hesitantly.

AJ's eyes looked downward upon hearing her request. "You were right, you know," he admitted. "I do regret not having said goodbye to either of them that day when they were still in the surgical room or just before the burial ceremony. I should have come down. I should have sat next to you then. I only heard a word or two of the ceremony. God, I was such a mess. I wish I could have that time back," AJ admitted.

So far, Erika liked what she was hearing but she was still waiting for his response to visit their graves.

"Yeah, Rik, I think that would be nice, and I'm glad you'll be there with me. I should have paid them the respect they deserved a long time ago," he admitted, patting her leg.

Erika smiled. That was exactly what she wanted to hear. Now, they could begin the rest of their lives together. From that point on, Erika knew she had her true husband back. She knew she'd be able to count on him, and they'd be stronger after what they'd overcome. Erika believed what Dr. Pap had said about "from the hurt, you find the healing."

The Embera Village were eager to welcome Erika and AJ home. The first night they were there, a celebration was held both for their reunion and their return. AJ was worried for a moment that they thought the couple would be there permanently, but Ratu eased his concern. The Embera understood it was just a visit, but were happy they were there, nonetheless. AJ took a couple hours to answer some questions for Dr. Roman and two of the new docs he'd brought on. AJ felt comfortable with Dr. Roman's choices and felt confident with handing the torch over to them. He felt like Dr. Pap would have approved as well. Erika was happy to finally meet Dr. Roman and thanked him for the work he did with Luke, who was thrilled to her about Luke's first game back. He agreed that a first game comeback like that was nothing short of a miracle.

Erika was nervous as they walked the path leading to where Dr. Pap and Kunu had been laid to rest. She kept an eye on AJ's facial expressions, but he was calm and collected. They cleaned up the area around where they were buried and surprisingly, AJ poured out his heart to both of them. AJ promised to make Dr. Pap proud by continuing to make a difference as he did, and he promised him that he'll continue to do what's hard and to have faith in himself. AJ told Kunu that when he sees him again in heaven, that he expects him to have his jump shot down. He also asked him to be a good "angel-example" to Dr. Pap's young son up there in heaven. Erika said silent prayers but let them know how much she loved and missed them. The couple spent a long time paying their respects and each felt very good about their visit.

They'd begun walking the path back towards the village when they saw Ratu running towards them calling, "Ms. Erika, Ms. Erika, Dr. Benjamin, phone call. Ms. Erika, you need to take this phone call right now!" he said, hardly able to breath.

"Okay, Okay, Ratu, calm down, just calm down," she told him as she took the phone from him, staring at AJ utterly confused.

"Hello," she said.

"Mom! Mom!" Luke said, panic stricken.

"What's wrong, Luke? Just try and calm down," Erica said, trying to help him pull it together.

Erika quickly removed the cell phone from her ear and placed the call on speaker phone so AJ could hear what was going on as well.

"Mom, Evie's missing," he said.

"Missing? What do you mean she's missing?" Erika asked him, now starting to freak out herself.

"I mean, she never made it to Tokyo," Luke clarified. "We booked two different flights but for the same day. I got here two days ago, and I just assumed Evie was with Joel or whatever until he called me looking for her," Luke explained. "She should have been here by now, Mom. She's not answering her cell phone either," he said, now increasingly hysterical.

AJ put his arm around his wife as they listened and Ratu began to pray.

"Luke," Erika said authoritatively, "I want you to call the police and make a report. Tell them just what you told me, every detail. I want you to call the airport in Tokyo and see if she's picked up her bags. Call your dad and see when he talked to her last.

"Luke," Erica continued, "if you want to find your sister, you're going to have to keep your head on and stay as calm as you can. Write down absolutely everything you can remember, even if it seems irrelevant. AJ and I are on our way."

The three of them ran back to the Embera Village, said a quick goodbye, grabbed their things, and they were booked on the next flight to Tokyo.

www.ingramcontent.com/pod-product-compliance
Lightning Source LLC
Chambersburg PA
CBHW050519190726
48284CB00003B/874